The Waters of Nyr

A Novel

Terrie Leigh Relf

The Waters of Nyr
by Terrie Leigh Relf

Cover design by Atomic Fly Studios

First Printing, August 2011

Sam's Dot Publishing
P.O. Box 782
Cedar Rapids, Iowa, 52406-0782 USA
www.samsdotpublishing.com
e-mail: sdpshowcase@yahoo.com

To my mother,
Constance Kay Freeman Relf,
who just left Earth to embark on her next grand adventure.

Author's Notes and Acknowledgments

No book, or any other piece of writing, is born in a vacuum. There are so many people I would like to thank, without whom this book would not have come into being.

James B. Baker, the founder of ProMart, now Sam's Dot Publishing, my mentor, my friend, who continues to inspire me from whatever realm of the space-time continuum he currently inhabits.

Tyree Campbell, the Managing Editor of Sam's Dot Publishing, without whom it would not have been finished. A few years ago, when I abandoned the story, he commanded me in no uncertain terms to FINISH IT!

And here I thought it would end up lining his cockatiel cage!

Edward Cox, who graciously assisted me while I thrashed about in plotting hell, and who encouraged me to keep at it, despite my many tantrums.

My grandmother, Delonto Mae Relf, who first introduced me to Erich Van Daniken's seminal work, *Chariots of the Gods;* my grandmother Florence Freeman, for passing on her writing genes; my parents, Constance Kay Relf and Geoffrey Clark Relf, for a truly creative home environment (not to mention those genes); my brother, Kirk Cary Relf, who continues to encourage and believe in me; my godfather Seymore Goodman, a former NASA metallurgist, who has taught me much about science and politics, and who has shared countless wonder-filled books, including Asimov's and Clarke's; my Hauran spawn, Brandon and Willow, both of whom inspire me daily. I also need to thank Willow for her editorial assistance, and far be it for me to argue with her, as she has already predicted that it will be a movie!

Whom does she want to play? The Barista from the Star Gazer Café, of course. I'll have to ask Brandon where he sees himself within "all this". Speaking of playing, perhaps he can compose—or play on—the soundtrack? Make an appearance as a drummer somewhere within the film?

Me? I've always wanted to play a shape-shifting monster, so thank you, Ed, for that crunchy bit!

Last, but certainly not least, sozar to everyone who encouraged me to keep at this ongoing saga. You are all Honorable Friends of Boort!

For those of you who have read *The Ice Queen,* my illustrated story book (Sam's Dot, 2005?), "Sisters of the Blood Moon", which appeared in *Hungur Magazine's* Issue 9, and "The Rim of Sorrows" in David Lee Summers' *Tales of the Talisman* (winter 2010), this novel touches on those universes. Then there's *The Drabbler*.

While gestating this novel and its spin-offs, a number of Boortean universe poems, micro fictions, and short stories have appeared in such publications as the *Flashshot Daily Genre Fiction* pieces.

Humbly Yours,
The Boortean Ambassador to Haura
Terrie Leigh Relf

We tell bedtime stories to children so that they may learn the truth of who they are.
—A Mahrainian Saying

Chapter 1

Cassandra dipped her paint brush into the murky water, swathed it around in the crimson paint. *Yes, paint the sun just so behind the moons, illuminating them against this strange indigo night.*

"Cassie—that's quite the painting. One of a series it seems." Ms. Brunhof tapped a finger alongside her chin, studying her young student's painting. *Moons and stars and strange planetary configurations. This one should be an astronomer instead of an artist.*

There was something familiar, though, about these configurations. This wasn't the first time an image revealed by Cassie's pencil or brush had quickened something stored within Ms. Brunhof's mind. She studied Cassie for a moment, noted how her pale skin looked even paler with those thick locks of honey-brown hair. And those odd violet eyes. . .where had she seen eyes like that before? The memory eluded Ms. Brunhof, who realized her mind was wandering much too often lately.

Cassie sighed, swizzled her brush in the water again before drying it off on a clean rag. She twisted the rag between small, but elegant, hands, then tossed it on her work table.

"I just can't seem to get the lighting right. There's this burst of color in my mind but it's subtle too, and it comes from behind the two moons illuminating the third and—"

"Cassie, slow down, "Ms. Brunhof chuckled, smoothing unruly red hair away from her eyes when she leaned over to peer a bit closer. "It's a work-in-process. Take your time. Why not work on the still life I set up like the rest of the class?" She tilted her head toward the room's center, where there was a table draped with a piece of burlap and several avocados. The other students, whose easels formed a semi-circle around the table, were intently studying the objects, some painting furiously. Cassie cringed as one student drug his easel toward her, the sound of the metal-tipped wood legs against the old linoleum more than a bit unnerving.

"Ok. But I keep seeing this image. It pops into my mind all the time. I just have to make it right."

"I understand, Cassie. But perhaps you need to take a break from it. I think you're trying too hard."

"Avocados?" she grimaced.

"Yes, and make them green, ok?" Ms. Brunhof smiled consolingly. She really didn't mind teaching art, as it took her mind off other matters—especially how bored she had become of late. While art hadn't been her first choice of subjects to teach, for the most part, she found observing their process to be intriguing. It provided her with insights into how they thought, how they interpreted their collective environment—and their mental landscapes—on the page.

"Ok, all right. Green avocados," Cassie paused to look at them for a moment, grimaced. "I can't stand them, though. They make me want to vomit."

One of the other students started laughing. Ms. Brunhof turned to look at him. What was his name again? Oh yes, Baron. Now there's another promising student, Ms. Brunhof thought, but he tended to be a low-achiever. She really had no patience for people who didn't give their all, and yet, she couldn't help but be amused by him at times. Even though she wasn't an adept artist herself, she could definitely see that he was gifted. Probably why he didn't work that hard at it. It was too easy for him. He needed a challenge. Constant challenges was probably more like it, she mused. She could relate to that, too. . .more so than her students could possibly imagine.

Ms. Brunhof sighed louder than she intended. One of her headaches was coming on. Another student, Meagan, turned around to glare at Cassie and Baron who were chattering back-and-forth.

"Shhhh—some of us are trying to work here," Meagan called out, the irritation clear in her voice. Ms. Brunhof nodded in approval. Meagan smiled, resumed painting. Ms. Brunhof respected discipline—and order. She much preferred it when students monitored each other. It left her free to focus on more important matters.

"They make me hurl, too." He thrust out his hand. "Name's Baron, but people call me Bare."

"Cassandra," she said, wondering why she hadn't noticed him before, as he was nearly six-feet tall, and even though she wouldn't call him buffed-out, he barely fit in the studio chair. He had blue-black hair with a bit of a wave in it that hung just above his shoulders. Such friendly eyes, too, with several shades of green all vying for attention.

"But people always seem to call me Cassie. Aren't avocados disgusting?"

Baron kept smiling at Cassie, and she noticed that he had dimples. She loved his dimples and that lop-sided grin.

"That's enough from you two. Paint!" Ms. Brunhof readjusted her thick metal-rimmed glasses. She made a mental note to order a stronger pair. The light in this studio was just too bright, and she was tired of the headaches. Her three back-to-back "Introduction to Studio Arts" classes seemed to drag on today. She'd been here in San Diego much too long, she thought, feeling the irritation, and a touch of anger, mounting. Much too long. And for what?

"Yes, Ms. Brunhof," Baron and Cassie chanted in unison.

Ms. Brunhof tried to look stern—even placed both hands on her somewhat ample hips—but failed miserably. "I don't know why I didn't think of pairing you two up before. Two pearls in a shell."

Cassie and Baron studied each other for a moment, then laughed. Yes, there was something to what Ms. Brunhof said, they both thought. Almost as if they recognized each other.

But from where?

Baron and Cassie both shrugged, returned to painting.

Back at her desk, Ms. Brunhof watched Cassie and Baron. Yes, there was something about those two. They even resembled each other in a vague way. Something around the eyes, the jaw lines. Their coloring was quite different, though. While Baron's hair was midnight black, Cassie's was honey-brown. Where Cassie had pale luminescent skin, Baron's had dark undertones. While Baron's eyes were green, Cassie's were an unusual shade of purple. Who had purple eyes? They were probably contacts, Ms. Brunhof realized. No one on this planet had that shade naturally, did they?

The resemblance, she noted, was in the shape of their eyes. Slavic? Asian? Something in-between, she mused, like that recent photo exhibit she'd seen of Laplanders, or Saami, as they preferred to be called.

One of the few pleasures Ms. Brunhof allowed herself were trips to the local museums and galleries. Even though she knew better, being stuck in this dismal town still felt like a demotion. She sighed as another wave of pain, the second this morning, threatened to undo her good mood. Ten minutes between classes wasn't enough time to deal with her throbbing head, so she grabbed her satchel and ran out of the classroom.

* * *

Thirty minutes later, when Ms. Brunhof still hadn't returned to class, most of the students cleaned up their stuff and left. Cassie and Baron lingered a bit.

"I hope she's okay," Cassie said, glancing around the quad for a sign of her return.

Baron shrugged, said, "Wanna go for coffee?"

"Sorry, Bare. Maybe another time. I need to help my grandmother sort through more boxes. We just moved here before the semester started, and there are ten-thousand things to do still."

"I've got a Grams that eats up all my time, too. We moved here a few months ago, and we still haven't unpacked everything. Maybe this weekend then? Here's my e-mail, my cell, and my home phone—or you could beep me!"

He handed her a card. She turned it back and forth a few times. "Funny. Invisible ink or something?"

"Or something. I'm loads of fun. Give me a chance and I'll prove it to you." He grabbed the card from her, then wrote down his digits, handed it back to her.

Cassie tore the corner off one of her wadded-up drawings, scribbled her phone and e-mail, then shoved it in his hand.

"See ya later then—oh, Cassie."

Cassie turned around, looked at him expectantly.

"Why don't you bring your drawing pad. We could sketch together or something. You know, for the portfolio?"

"Sure—see you later!" Cassie sang, rushing a bit now so she didn't miss her bus. Otherwise, she'd have to wait for thirty or more minutes, and she always got fidgety waiting. She'd rather walk, but she had all her art supplies and book bag.

"Oh, and Cassie. . .I see those three moons sometimes. I have these ah—dreams."

She whirled around to face him, her full lips forming a little "o". "Really? That is too weird—but cool at the same time." She cocked her head to study him.

Baron grinned. He hadn't been sure whether he should say anything or not. It was nice to meet someone he connected with, and most people his age usually thought he was some kind of nerd, which he supposed he was, but still. . .it wasn't like dreaming about three moons was all that bizarre. Didn't Jupiter have five or something? It kept changing, though, so he made a mental note to look it up later, then realized he still hadn't set up his computer. He and his Grams had moving down to a science, but that didn't mean he liked to unpack and put things away. He'd rather just spend time drawing or hanging out at The Star Gazer café.

Chapter 2

The bus—and Cassie—were in sync, which heightened her good spirits. She was still humming a quirky little tune that seemed to be set on "repeat" in her mind as she opened the screen door, let it bounce until it closed behind her.

"My, you're in a good mood this afternoon. I told you San Diego would agree with you." Grandmother Iliana gave Cassie her usual welcome-home hug, held her a bit longer than usual.

"I met someone in art class today. His name is Baron."

Gramma Iliana let her go. "Did you say 'Baron'?"

"Gramma, what's wrong? You look like you've seen a ghost."

"Not a ghost, sweetie. I just think I know his grandmother. Describe him."

"There you go again, Gramma. He lives with his grand-mother—what are the odds?"

"Describe him."

"Ok, he's about six feet, blue-black hair, green eyes—and oh, he hates avocados, too, and—"

"Is that so?" Iliana tucked a stray red hair behind her ear. She fixed her dark brown almond-shaped eyes on Cassie.

"Well, I do believe you've met my friend, Selene's, grandson." Her eyes misted over.

"Is something wrong, Gramma?" Cassie had forgotten to mention that Baron had dreams with three moons, too, but now probably wasn't the time.

"No honey, it's just this heat." She closed her eyes, tried to still the rapid beating of her heart. "I'll be right back. I need to get a glass of water, then make a phone call."

Cassie watched as her grandmother walked into the bedroom, closed and locked the door. She never used to lock the door. But hey, her Gramma gave her privacy, why shouldn't she do the same? Still, it was the timing. It wasn't that her Gramma didn't seem pleased that she'd met her friend's grandson, so there was probably another reason. It was hot, after all. Cassie sort of liked it, though, but in small doses. It reminded her of when they lived in Arizona. She loved how bright the stars were at night—almost as if you could reach out and pluck them from the sky. When she was little, she thought they were flowers, and her Gramma would hold her up so she could extend her chubby little hands into the sky to reach for them.

Baron's face popped into Cassie's mind, and she thought about calling him. What were the odds that she'd been drawn to him of all people—and their grandmothers were friends! Her Gramma would call it synchronicity, and never seemed to tire of pointing out the connections between people and places—even objects—whenever the opportunity presented itself.

Cassie couldn't deny she felt a little spark of recognition with Baron—or Bare, as he preferred to be called. A genuine connection. She had learned to trust those feelings over the years, albeit with considerable promptings from her Gramma Iliana. It was a gift, according to her Gramma, and her birthright—whatever that meant.

But still. . .Cassie wasn't a stranger to common sense, and **it** was telling her to hold off. Regardless, she sensed—no, she *knew*—that they would become friends.

Or something more. Something much, much more.

But what?

If Ms. Brunhof hadn't made her draw those yucky avocados today, would she have met Baron? Even though they were in the same class, she hadn't noticed him before. She'd been so tired since they moved, and hadn't felt like socializing. She'd usually sit off to the corner, or in the back of class. Come to think of it, she was a bit of a loner anyway. Even though Bare had been warm and friendly, she had the feeling—no, she knew—that they were kindred spirits. While he may be the proverbial class clown, it was probably to keep people at bay rather than to draw them toward him.

But maybe she had noticed him before—out of the corner of her eye or something. Was he always late? Did he leave after break? Seriously, how could she recognize someone she'd never met? It just didn't add up. Could she have dreamed him along with those moons and other stuff? Gramma Iliana would probably say it was that birthright thing again. One of these days, she wished her grandmother would give her more than a brief explanation about that, rather than going on and on and on about the herbs in the noxious teas she made—as if she'd ever be brewing those for herself!

Then again, maybe she'd noticed Baron around campus. Yes, that must be it. It was like she'd been reunited with an old friend. It felt natural to want to hang out with him. There wasn't anything romantic about it, not like she had *those* kinds of feelings. Cassie hoped they had even more in common, as it was about time she met someone she could connect to. What with all their moving, leaving before one semester ended, arriving late for the next one, she was almost always the odd girl out. Even though her grandmother occasionally seemed to feel bad about her not making any real friends, she had seemed almost relieved when Cassie stopped bothering to make any friends at all. They had each other, after all, and when Cassie was honest with herself, she realized that she preferred living a simple life so she could focus on her art work.

Cassie paused to consider whether Ms. Brunhof was playing matchmaker. No, she was just noticing the connection, and since she was an artist, she probably had the same gifts that Cassie did. Artists saw the world in a different way. She did so adore Ms. Brunhof with her quirky outfits like the one she wore today with red-and-black polka dot pants with a black-and-red-striped tank top. She definitely had her own style. . .

Yes, Ms. Brunhof was one of her favorite teachers of all time. The woman had only known her for a few weeks, and she already seemed to understand Cassie's quirks in a way no other teacher had—and there had been way too many teachers who hadn't been so patient. But college, she reminded herself, was definitely different. It was easier to disappear in a college classroom.

Cassie counted to seven on her fingers. Seven high schools in four years before they moved to San Diego. Sometimes, it felt like an adventure, but truth be told, she wondered what it would be like to stay in one area for longer then five or six months. She'd never really questioned why they had to move all the time. She'd asked once—just once—and her Gramma's eyes had looked so sad that she didn't have the heart to ask her again. It was just part of their life. A major part.

At one point, when she was in elementary school, she'd fantasized that they were gypsies. When she was in junior high, the thought that they might be in the Witness Protection Program seemed more likely. Eventually, she just started to accept moving as a fact of life. She still managed to graduate from high school with good grades, and here she was a freshman at Eucalyptus Grove Community College! Would she finish out the semester here? It was unlikely. . .That birthright thing again, she mused, and wondered what else it entailed.

Still. Yes, there was something about Baron. But why had Gramma Iliana gotten all weird on her? Maybe it was menopause or something. Yes, that was it.

But if their grandmothers were friends, why hadn't they met before?

That was the strangest thing of all.

Chapter 3

Baron opened the front door. He was just about to announce his arrival, when he heard his Grams, Selene, talking to someone on the phone—but in a language he'd never heard her speak before.

He had no idea his Grams could speak another language, and whatever it was, she spoke it like a native. What nationality were they anyway? He'd always thought his grandmother looked Norwegian or Slavic, what with her high cheekbones, silvery blond hair and those intense blue eyes. But he looked nothing like her—and that didn't sound like Norwegian, or any language he'd ever heard before. Maybe it was Finnish or something. He thought that pop star, Björk, or was it Björn, spoke Finnish.

It dawned on him that there was so much he didn't know about his Grams—or about his family. Where were they from again? There had only been the two of them for as long as he could remember. No aunts, uncles, parents. She said they'd all died around the time he was born. A horrible accident. So all he knew was his Grams, who had cared for him from birth. Even though she said he was her grandson, and not his mother, it was always her face in his mind when he thought of mother.

"Grams, I'm home!"

Silence. She continued to babble on in that foreign language. Deciding it must be private—and important—he shrugged off his backpack, set it down in the entryway, went to his room.

A few minutes later, she knocked on his bedroom door.

When Baron opened the door, his Grams reached for her hug. He never got tired of hugging his Grams. There was something about her hugs that seemed to suffuse him with warmth. But when she pulled away, he noticed there were tears threatening to spill from her eyes.

"Grams, what's up?"

"Oh, it's nothing," she dabbed at them with a tissue. "I'm just feeling like time passes much too quickly these days. Like we've been catapulted into the future and can't return. Just look at you—a grown man now."

"Oh, Grams!" He gave her another hug, patted her back. "I'm only eighteen—and you know I love you. I won't run off or anything."

"I know, sweetie. I know. Still. . .life has a way of changing when you least expect it."

"There you go getting all cryptic on me again, Grams."

"It's just the nature of life. Hungry? How was school? Make any new friends today?"

"How'd you know that? I didn't have a chance to tell you. Are you in my head again, Grams? I'd prefer it if you'd knock before you opened the door."

Selene chuckled at their little joke. "Come into the kitchen while I make dinner."

"Yeah, I met this girl named Cassie in Ms. Brunhof's class. We're going to have coffee or something this weekend."

"How nice you two finally met," Selene said, opening the fridge. She pulled out the vegetable drawer, slammed it shut, scanned the contents of the meat and cheese drawer, scooted that closed, then spent an inordinate amount of time just staring into the fridge at nothing in particular. She reached for last night's leftover casserole, realizing she didn't have the energy to make anything from scratch tonight.

"Yes, Cassie is the granddaughter of a dear friend of mine. That was her grandmother, Iliana, on the phone. You remember my talking about her, don't you?

"Yeah. She's from your hometown or something. How cool is that? It looks like Cassie and I are destined to be friends."

Selene reached out to give Baron another hug, took his hand instead, held it for a time. "Yes, this is way cool, as you say. Way cool. We'll have to have them over for dinner soon. I'll make something special."

Baron squeezed his grandmother's hand. "Need any help with dinner?"

"Just leftovers, honey. Why don't you get started on your homework, and then we'll eat."

Baron nodded, kissed her on the cheek, and went into his bedroom. It was just off the kitchen, and had probably been an add-on from the original house. He liked how it was connected, but somewhat separated, from the main house. There was a large wood deck, or platform, that opened into the back yard, which was a jungle of exotic plants, undulating vines, and his favorite, an old peppercorn tree. He was sure that his Grams had chosen this place because of the garden. Another added plus was that he could cut through the back yard to go to his favorite café, The Star Gazer, just a few blocks away.

Baron unlatched the French doors, pushed them open, then plopped down on his unmade bed covered in sketch pads and pencils of one kind or another. He flipped through one of the medium-sized pads, found a blank page, stared into the yard for a few moments, then began drawing.

Baron couldn't help but think about Professor Brunhof. She was okay, but he wasn't as into her as Cassie seemed to be. True, she seemed to be a serious art teacher, but she'd never shared any of her own work, which he found odd. Most of the other art teachers he'd studied with had always been eager to share their work, or if not eager, then it didn't take much prompting. Maybe she was working on a new series of pieces, and was one of those people who didn't like to talk about their process—or show their work—until it was ready for display.

Baron figured she was a sculptor, though. Her hands looked sort of misshapen, as if they'd been reconstructed after having one-too-many accidents with a chisel or something. Maybe she'd even smashed them working on stone or metal sculptures.

Ms. Brunhof wanted them to have a sizable portfolio by the end of the semester, and that meant he'd need to make at least two-to-three sketches a day in order to have one good one for the week. Maybe he was his own worse critic, but he liked to think he had a good eye.

One of the things he liked about Ms. Brunhof was that she was totally fixated on plants. Maybe it was because she'd grown up in the desert or something. New Mexico or Arizona. He couldn't remember where she'd told the class she was from. He and his Grams had stayed in Idyllwild briefly before they moved to San Diego. Even though it was an arty town, there were huge pine trees all around. He loved the scent of them. Most of the surrounding area was dry, dusty, and so hot that it had made his flesh crawl. It was bright, too, which really bothered his eyes; they itched when he was out in the sun too long, as if he had insects crawling around behind his sockets.

If Ms. Brunhof wanted lush vibrant plants, he'd draw and then paint them for her. Not that he didn't like foliage, but he wasn't much different than other students who wanted "A's". It was a good thing he could pretty much draw whatever he saw—even from memory. He barely had to look at the page to do it, would just look at the object and start transferring the image. He was ambidextrous, too, so he could, and did, go on for hours. His Grams usually had to knock several times when he was working on a project in his room. He called it "being in the zone", because he couldn't think of any other way to explain what would come over him.

Baron flipped the cover of one of his large pads of paper, reached for his favorite drawing pencil, began to sketch the morning glory vine that covered one side of the fence. He loved the way the light seemed to pool on the uplifted leaves, how the purple flowers reached for the late afternoon sun.

He sketched for over an hour before his Grams called him for dinner. Baron looked down at the piece he was working on before closing the book and was surprised to see that he had added a figure into the scene. He peered closer to the drawing, studied the person's features, realized that it was Cassie.

Chapter 4

After a fitful sleep, Cassie woke up before her alarm. Was it Thursday or Friday? Saturday? She rubbed the sleep from her eyes, stared at the monkey-faced clock on her nightstand that read 10:13a.m., then at the Monet Calendar just above it. It was Saturday, but for some reason, it felt like one of those Monday's where she'd pulled an all-nighter to finish an art project. Her cell phone started flashing and vibrating on the nightstand. She wondered who could be calling her this early. Most of her phone calls were from her grandmother, so who could it be?

Cassie looked at the phone number. Didn't recognize it. "Hello," she mumbled, still groggy with sleep.

"Hey, Cassie. It's Baron. Hope I didn't call too early."

Cassie paused, surprised to hear from him, then remembered through her early morning fog-brain that she'd given him her number after class the day before.

"No. It's okay. I just woke up."

"Did you sleep last night? I couldn't sleep more than a few hours at a time. This is totally unreal. I usually sleep like the dead."

Cassie was having trouble keeping up with Baron's animated chatter. She listened to him go on and on, then finally, after another long pause where he said, "Cassie—Cassie, you still there?" She managed to clear her head enough to say something.

"I slept okay, I guess. I've always had these weird sleep cycles. Strange dreams and nightmares—ever since I can remember."

"I get nightmares, too. Usually wake up with a major headache afterwards. Grams brews this noxious tea that tastes like someone took a you-know-what in it."

"My Gramma makes something like that, too. For my nerves. I get stressed easy, hurl a lot. Geez, this is sure appetizing morning conversation. You still want to have coffee?"

"Why don't we meet over at Star Gazer's? It's that café on B and 26th or something. It's around the corner from my place, so I could be there in a few."

"Ok. I know where it is. We live around 28th and B. What a coincidence. It looks like we're practically neighbors. In about an hour? I need to jump in the shower."

"That works. See you!"

* * *

An hour or so later, Cassie arrived at the Star Gazer. Even though she'd only been there once or twice, she really liked it. The walls in the main part of the café had starscapes painted on them. Maybe she'd ask if she could do a mural or something on one of the other walls.

Baron was at the counter, flirting with a zombied-out barista. Cassie didn't feel the least bit jealous, and realized that must be because she and Bare were just going to be friend-friends—not that had any of those other feelings, but still, she'd wondered at first, if that was why they'd been so drawn to each other. She'd never had a boyfriend before, and her Gramma didn't encourage her in that direction. When the topic came up on occasion, her grandmother would always say, "There's time enough for that when you're on your own."

"On my own?" she always replied. "Are you kicking me out, Gramma?" They'd both laugh, and her grandmother would rest a hand on her cheek, say, "never!" Cassie couldn't imagine not living with her grandmother, but she knew in the way that she often knew things, that her life wasn't going to follow a normal path. What that meant, she had no idea, though, and so didn't dwell on it much. There was so much else to occupy her anyway, what with school and her art.

The café was practically empty, except for this huge buffed-out guy sitting in the corner who occasionally looked up from his i-pod. He had a smooth-shaved head and was wearing a thick leather jacket, with dark sunglasses, which Cassie thought was odd, seeing as it was probably 80 degrees outside and he was sitting inside, where it was probably ten degrees hotter. She tried not to stare, but couldn't help looking at him. For some reason, those shades bothered her. Perhaps it was because they seemed so out-of-place indoors and she couldn't see his eyes. He didn't frighten her, but his presence definitely made her feel a bit on-edge, as if something was about to happen. Even the air around him seemed to crackle with energy, like he had a force-field around him or something.

"There you are, Cassie!" Baron called out, motioning for her to join him at the counter. He turned back to the barista, said, "I'll have an Asteroid Blaster and one of those cookies. Cassie? My treat. What do you want?"

"I need a Blaster, too. Large. No food. My stomach is twisting around like a snake in a feeding frenzy."

The barista measured out several scoops of espresso, packed it into the strainers, fitted them into the machine, flipped the switch.

Cassie watched the thick elixir burble down into the cups.

"Yum. Where you wanna sit?" Cassie glanced around the room, noticed that the buffed-out guy was still sitting in the corner. He looked up and directly at them. The corner of one side of his mouth twitched, like he was almost smiling. She tried to be polite, to smile back at him, but her face was still slack from a lack of restful sleep, so she just nodded. He turned away and went pack to his i-pod, or whatever it was.

"Let's sit out back in the patio. It's totally empty. Find a seat. They just turned on the misters, too, so it'll be cooler. I'll bring the coffee." Baron noticed the guy in the corner, too, paused to look at him for a moment, then turned away. He felt the guy's eyes on him, thought about turning around again, saying something—what, he didn't know—then decided not to. There was something familiar about that guy. He never forgot a face, just couldn't always place them in the right context. Probably a regular, Baron thought. Just a regular. Still, there was something about the guy that tugged at his memories.

"Here—" The Barrista handed him a tray loaded down with their drinks and a plate piled high with cookies.

"You gonna eat all those!" Cassie exclaimed as he made his way toward their table beneath the bougainvillea, careful not to brush up against the jutting thorns.

"Something for your snake's next feeding frenzy."

Cassie's stomach growled in response. "I can't stand food in the morning, but hey, it's almost noon, and they do look good. I love lemon bars."

"They call them something else here. Star Ooze or Star Dust. That's why I just point." Baron grinned, took a bite out of one of the lemon bars.

"I brought one of my portfolios. I wanted to show you some of my sketches, see what you think. You may think I'm a weirdo, but I'm totally fixated on those three moons. I swear there should be three—rather than one—in the night sky."

She set the large leather folio on the table between them, unzipped it.

Baron slid closer, took a bite of his lemon bar, then almost choked on it as Cassie peeled back the first page of her portfolio.

"What? You recognize this? It's one of the first drawings in this series. I used to dream about these landscapes, wander through them. Then, about five years ago, I just started drawing them. I'd always been into art. Gramma loves to paint, too, but she mainly does ocean scenes that look like they're local, if you get my drift."

Baron leaned over Cassie's drawing, traced the curves and spires of the alien landscape with his finger over the plastic. "I've seen this place. There are caves over there, behind that rock face."

"Caves? Wait a minute—" Cassie flipped through the book until she came to a sketch of a cave filled with crystal formations. "Like this—"

"Yes—I get trapped there in my dreams sometimes. They go down hundreds of feet beneath the surface. It's like a maze. One time, though, I woke up in the dream, you know, like a lucid dream, and I managed to think more clearly, not just stumble through in a panic. I came-to in a huge cavern. It pulses with this weird light—then whoosh, I was awake, and Grams was there with that rancid tea. It's like she knows what I'm dreaming."

"That is too weird."

"Now that we know our families go way back, I'm thinking we used to play together when we were little." Baron reached for his Blaster, took a swig, smacked his lips. "Next time, you should try a Black Hole. It's loaded with chocolate syrup."

Cassie nodded, sipping her Blaster. "Maybe we saw the same scary movies on TV. I used to watch the History and Discovery Channel and stuff with my Gramma all the time. You don't have to go very far to find strange stuff on this planet."

Baron didn't respond, just kept staring at the page, sorting through images that continued to rise in his mind. Cassie turned to the next page, then the next. They were so engrossed with looking at Cassie's portfolio, that they didn't notice the leather-jacketed guy had been watching them while standing just outside the patio door, partially hidden by an assortment of hanging ferns and other plants, entering something into his hand-held computer.

Over the next few hours, Cassie and Baron looked through the portfolio, chatting about their day-to-day lives, noting how it all seemed to piece together with an odd assortment of coincidences, just like an abstract collage.

"Who's that?" Baron pointed to a male figure sitting on a rock face looking out on a blue-green ocean.

"Oh, him. Yeah. I don't know. He started to pop into my mind recently. I never see much more than his profile. I have more of him in another portfolio."

"Pops into your mind? You mean like contacts you telepathically? Grams does that all the time. We've always joked about it. Now I wonder."

"My Gramma says seeing things more clearly is my birthright. I don't know if I'm psychic or whatever, but sometimes, I just know whether things are true or not. She's really sensitive to my moods, too, says it's because she loves me. I wonder. . .It's sort of freaky and weird, isn't it?"

"Weird is often my middle name, Cass. Tell me more about this guy. . ."

"Well, it's like we share a mind or something. No, it's not like that, really. I sense him, though. I see film reels of him walking along the beach, or whatever this place is. I don't usually see people when I draw or paint. Just landscapes. Buildings. Space stuff."

"He's connected to all this. I'm sure of it." Baron reached for his Blaster. It was cold, but he downed it anyway

"Think so?" Cassie started to reach for another cookie, then changed her mind. She wasn't ready for food yet.

"Know so. Hey Cass, it's almost three. We should probably head home. What's your Grams making for dinner?"

"I don't know, but hey—did you ever wonder why you move so much?"

"Yeah," Baron said, gathering cookie crumbs into a pile before brushing them into his hand, then tossing them onto the ground for the birds. "Another one of those weird coincidences with us, eh? We're supposed to have dinner together soon. Grams said she'd make something special." He smacked his lips in anticipation of one of his grandmother's special meals. She would go all out for company. Maybe even make those little potatoes cooked with butter, sugar, and cinnamon.

A chair scraped across the floor, startling Cassie. She whisked her head around to see the leather-jacket guy leaving the café by a side door through the patio.

"That guy almost gives me the creeps," Cassie whispered to Baron, whose eyes narrowed to slits.

"Yeah, me, too." Baron glanced out the window to see the guy climb into some sort of jeep, then peel away from the curb.

Chapter 5

It was a somewhat gloomy Monday, but the early morning gray would probably rearrange into clear blue skies with the usual brush-stroked clouds. Cassie turned away from the window, grabbed her new pink hoodie, and was almost out the door when Baron called.

"Wanna ride?" He pulled the cell away from his ear as she squealed, "Sure!" despite just downing the rest of one of her grandmother's teas. She didn't want to miss class again, as Ms. Brunhof promised they'd do collages today. Cassie loved to make collages, and over the years, she'd collected several boxes of pictures and postcards, different types of paper, scraps of fabric and bits and pieces of this and that. If it weren't for the fact that she always seemed to run out of glue, she'd probably have more collages than wall space.

"How soon before you're here?"

"I'm right outside. Grams gave me the address—and oh, we're all having dinner at our place tonight. It's already planned."

"Cool—see you in a sec." Cassie closed her phone, stuck it in her denim packback, which she slung over her shoulder. When she was little, she mixed up her P's and B's, and still called her backpack, packback. As with all her other quirks, this one also seemed to linger. It had something to do with her headaches, she knew—or at least that's what she thought her Gramma had said.

"I'm leaving, Gramma!" Cassie called out. "Baron said we're having dinner at his house tonight."

Iliana came out from the kitchen with a thermos for Cassie. "Oh Gramma—not for school!" She whined, imagining the disgusted expressions on her classmates' face when the thermos was opened—not to mention her breath!

"It's cocoa, sweetie. Just cocoa. Extra cinnamon." Iliana "tsk-tsked", pressing it into Cassie's hands. "Have a good day—and yes, dinner at Selene's tonight. You will really like her." She leaned down so Cassie could kiss her on the cheek.

"Okay, Gramma." "Baron's outside waiting. I better go."

* * *

Ms. Brunhof was definitely not in a good mood this morning. Cassie noticed that her art teacher's brows furrowed every so often as if she were in pain, and while she wasn't unattractive, this gesture made her look really odd and misshapen, almost as if she'd been in a bad car wreck and had plastic surgery that hadn't quite healed up right.

"We better behave ourselves today," Cassie whispered to Baron while Ms. Brunhof gestured to the back tables where there were bins of supplies. "Get creative!" she said. "Among other things, I'll be grading you on texture and form. . ." her voice trailed off as she grabbed her head, groaned. She leaned over to pick up her satchel with effort, then headed out the door.

"There she goes again," Cassie said, frowning, her concern obvious. "I'm wondering if she gets migraines, too?"

"I think she has eye trouble. Do you notice how she's always wearing those prescription shades in class? Maybe she has that light sensitivity thing. She'll be back."

"Still. . ."Cassie stared out the front doors, which were left open in hopes of a breeze and to allow more light to enter the studio classroom. It was going to be another hot day despite the early morning gloom, so Cassie was relieved she'd worn shorts and a tank-top. The hoodie was balled up in her packback just in case.

A lot of students didn't show up today, and were probably at the beach or the park. Ms. Brunhof had been promising them a field trip to the downtown Harbor to see the public art installations once the heat wave dissipated. She was really looking forward to going on The Star of India, too. Cassie sighed, wishing she was on a harbor cruise or something, then remembered how sea sick she got. Sea sick. Car sick. Bus sick. She was always better off on solid ground on her own two feet. Flying was okay, though. The few times that they'd traveled by plane had been awesome. She really liked taking off, feeling the plane pierce through the air, attaining altitude before leveling off. Then, she'd just gaze out the window at the clouds, amazed at how she felt suspended in time, nearly motionless, even though they were going thousands of miles per hour.

When they'd moved to California from Arizona, Cassie and her grandmother had taken an evening flight. Even through the trip only lasted an hour or so, it was more than enough time for her to be inspired by the view of the city at night. It reminded her of something, but of what, she wasn't sure.

She looked over at Baron who was riffling through bins, but didn't seem to find anything he liked. He looked at Cassie, shrugged, grabbed a handful of paper scraps without even looking at them. "It's way too hot to be indoors. I wish I was home lying underneath my peppercorn tree."

"That sounds nice," she whispered back, returned to her seat, her hands full of fabric scraps and what felt like hand-made paper.

Their classmates were on the quiet side today. All that Cassie and Baron could hear was the tearing of paper mingled with the sounds of shuffling through bins of beads and buttons, corks and bottle caps. Occasionally, someone fought over a choice bit of paper or fabric, but in general, they were all busy working on their collages. When Ms. Brunhof finally returned to class, she looked a bit better, but her skin still seemed pulled too tight around her forehead. Baron wondered if she'd had a bad facelift for a moment, then abandoned that thought. She just had a headache. A really bad headache, he told himself, still amazed at how pain could distort it so much, as if she were wearing a mask over another, more slender face.

"That's it!" he exclaimed in a loud whisper to Cassie. "I'm going to make a mask!" and he was off to explore the contents of various bins for what he needed.

"Whatever," she sighed, not turning away from the alien landscape taking form in front of her. Ms. Brunhof came by, glanced at her work, then did a double-take. "It looks like a topographical map," she said.

"Really?" Cassie turned the piece this way and that. "You're right. It does sort of look like a map—but to what?"

"Something for you to discover, Cassie. And it looks like you're well on your way." Ms. Brunhof attempted a smile, which almost traveled up to her eyes.

"I hope you feel better. I get horrendous headaches, too, you know."

Ms. Brunhof seemed to perk up at that. "Really? I'm so sorry to hear that. I thought living closer to the beach would relieve them. Instead, it seems to be making them worse."

Cassie nodded in sympathy, then studied Ms. Brunhof's face for awhile, noticed that many of the lines had smoothed out, but her eyes were still all puffy. If she'd had plastic surgery before, they'd done a pretty good job. Not spectacular, but pretty good. Close-up, Cassie could see a few furrows on the side of Ms. Brunhof's face that were only slightly covered by her unruly curls.

"My Grandmother makes me these teas. It helps sometimes. Mostly sleep works, though—and doing art work. It's like it takes me to a different place, to dreamtime or something."

"Or something," Ms. Brunhof replied, her mind still reeling with pain-clouded thoughts—but there was a glimmer of something else in there. Relief? Even her eyes looked less puffy.

Chapter 6

The door bell rang around 7:30pm. Gramma Selene answered it while Baron sat in the kitchen's breakfast nook waiting. He rolled and unrolled one of the napkins as if each time he unrolled it, something other than a napkin would be revealed—or perhaps an answer to the unformulated question that had been jarred loose and was rising to the surface, like so much muck in a pond.

It was probably the dreams. . . Ever since the semester began, he'd been having dreams in three-dimensions. There were pieces of a map—like Cassie's topo in class earlier today, which shifted this way and that as if he were manipulating them on a computer. But he hadn't been using a computer in the dream; he'd been using his fingers to point and draw, to drag and place, each section of the map that was suspended in midair. While he didn't play video games, the dream reminded him of being inside a 3-D video game.

"Hey, Bare," Cassie called out as she walked through the front door into the living room.

"I'm in here—in the kitchen!" he called back, scooting his chair away from the wood table. "Be right out," he called, pushing the chair back against the table, trying to rearrange his mood for company. He'd been looking forward to this night—to their all having dinner together—so why was he feeling so out-of-it?

Bare walked into the living room, waved at Cassie, then plopped down on the couch. Cassie sat down next to him. "Help yourself," he said, reaching toward a plate of fruit. Cassie reached for what first appeared to be a bunch of grapes, plucked one, then peeled back the thick red skin before popping them it into her mouth. Juice dribbled down her chin. "Ummmm. Seedless." She grabbed another handful, ate one after another until she sighed, then leaned back on the comfy sofa cushions.

"The Grammsies are still in the back yard, gathering herbs or something. I don't think they've even started dinner yet, but they're certainly in a good mood. It's like they haven't seen each other in ages, but we know better." He turned toward Cassie, looked into her eyes. They looked a bit swollen. She noticed his concern.

"Just a little headache again. I'm better, though. It's like I'm getting them more often or something. Weird, eh?" Cassie kicked him playfully. "They talk on the phone enough, though. Wouldn't it be weird if we were related?" Cassie cocked her head to study Baron. She didn't see anything that would tell her they were. Not a thing.

"Our Grammsies go way back, it seems. Hey—have you ever heard your Gram speak another language? They were talking in it on the phone. Totally weird. I'd never heard her speak anything but English. I didn't recognize it, either. Nothing I ever heard before. I thought it was Finnish at first, but I'm not sure."

"Me, neither. We should ask them. What's keeping them? The suspense is killing me."

"Yeah. Baron grabbed a slice of what looked like melon, but no melon they'd had before. He wondered where his Grams got all this fruit. It was definitely not their usual fare. Probably something from the Farmers Market she went to occasionally in North Park.

"Do you have any uncles, aunts, or anything—and where's your parents?" Baron asked.

"Died around the time I was born. There's just us. We move around a lot, too. My Gramma calls it 'exploring the universe', but lately, I've wondered if she's trying to protect me from something."

"Or someone." Baron chewed thoughtfully. "I'm going to pour us some sweet tea. Grams made it special for today."

Left alone in the living room, Cassie looked around. Nothing on the walls. No photos or paintings. There was a built-in bookshelf, but the only thing on it was a set of keys. No books or other knick-knacks. Maybe they hadn't even unpacked yet.

Cassie's Grandmother had insisted they get right to work making their house a home. She'd hung up several of her own paintings as well as a few of Cassie's. One of her Grandmother's seascapes was hanging on the wall behind the couch. It was an old painting that had always hung behind their couch since she was little. Just inside the foyer, there was a more recent picture her grandmother had painted when they'd returned from a short trip to Idyllwild. It was a desert landscape at twilight, rocks casting eerie shadows. They'd spent a week or so there before settling into San Diego. Cassie was glad they hadn't moved there as the weather was way too hot.

A few of Cassie's paintings hung just outside her bedroom in the hall. They were her usual attempts to recapture dreamscapes: three moons in the night sky, a planet below burgeoning with odd-looking structures and unusual plants. To the side, and almost off-canvas, caves, hidden from view. Beyond these, she always sensed there was water.

There was another painting that her grandmother had insisted upon hanging, even though Cassie knew it wasn't finished. It was the entrance to one of the caves. She'd laid down enough paint to suggest the opening and what lay just beyond the entrance, but so much of the off-white canvas showed through her hesitant brush strokes that it didn't look at all like the cave in her recurring dreams. It was another cave altogether, but how it related to the other dreams and drawings, she wasn't sure.

"Think of it this way," her Grandmother said, "every time you pass by, you'll see into the space—and more of the scene will reveal itself to you. It's a discovery process."

At the time, Cassie had agreed with her Grandmother, had actually thought it was a good idea. But now, after hanging there for over a month, passing it more times than she could count, the scene had not unveiled itself to her. If anything, the images were less clear than when she started painting them.

"There you are, dear!" Cassie's Grandmother Iliana came into the living room leading Bare's Grams by the hand. She got up from the couch, and before she had found her balance, was grasped tightly in Gramma Selene's arms. "It's so good to see you again, sweetie!" She squeezed Cassie close against her for the longest time, and even though Cassie wasn't used to being touched by anyone but her own Grandmother, it felt familiar—and wonderful.

They all chuckled as Grandma Selene finally released Cassie and she wobbled a bit. Bare reached out to keep her from falling back on the couch. As Cassie looked from one Grandmother to the next, their eyes crinkled with delight, she thought they bore a resemblance, like cousins, perhaps, if not sisters. They both had silver hair with blue-black undertones, but her Gramma liked to leave hers loose and flowing down her back, while Bare's grandmother wore hers twisted into a chignon, and fastened with a beautiful abalone hair stick. Their eyes weren't quite the same color, either, but they were the same height and slender.

The feeling passed after a few moments, and Cassie realized that she had seen what she wanted to see, as she so wanted them all to be a family. The odd thing is that she'd never fixated on wanting a family beyond what she and her Gramma shared. So many new thoughts and feelings seemed to be emerging since Bare had come into her life. And her dreams were affected as well, as if their meeting was a catalyst, and she was only now beginning to sense what that might mean. If this evening was a preview of what was to come, she was all for it. She smiled at her Gramma, Bare's Grams, then Bare. They all stood there grinning for the longest time before the grandmothers shifted the mood.

“Dinner in about an hour. Why don’t you show Cassie your room, Baron. We’ll talk over dinner.”

“Sure—come on, Cass. You’re going to love my back porch deck thingie.”

Chapter 7

After the unbearable heat, fall came early, and with it, a different kind of warmth descended upon San Diego. Baron, Cassie, and their grandmothers now shared meals, usually dinner, several nights a week. On Saturdays and Sundays, Cassie and Baron worked on their portfolios together on his back porch, while their grandmothers put in a late fall and winter garden. It seemed like Cassie had been hasty in her initial assessment; they were definitely settling in, and even Bare's grandmother had unpacked all of her boxes.

While Gramma Selene didn't seem to stockpile stuff like she and her grandmother did, there were definitely more homey touches in the living room. A hand-woven red-and-purple throw rug in front of the burnt orange corduroy comfy chair, pots of ferns and other houseplants—even a simply-framed pencil drawing of the garden—was hanging over their matching sofa.

The scent of a spicy vegetable soup wafted through the house, and Cassie's stomach rumbled as she reached for a pencil sharpener.

"Dinner won't be long." Grandmother Selene poked her head into Baron's room. "Time to wash up."

"Okay, Grams," Baron said, pushing his sketch board to the side. "Just leave everything out. Maybe we'll work on it tomorrow."

"Okay." Cassie said. "It's probably going to rain—that'll be cool. I love the rain. Maybe I'll add it to my picture." She glanced down at one of her portfolio pieces. It was yet another attempt to do something other than her usual dreamscapes: Bare's garden and peppercorn tree. She wondered how the picture would shift if it rained. The branches would hang lower, droop, and the red peppercorns would scatter around the yard. She hoped Ms. Brunhof would like it.

Selene was pouring tea as Baron and Cassie came into the kitchen. The soup smelled incredible. "A recipe from home," she said, ladling it into large ceramic soup bowls, then setting one in front of Cassie, then Baron, then Iliana, before carrying a bowl to where she was sitting.

"And there's fresh-baked bread, too!" Baron exclaimed, reaching for a thick slice. It wasn't any kind of bread Cassie had ever seen. Her grandmother usually made muffins chocked full of stuff that tasted too healthy. There was also a plate of assorted cheeses, some of which made Cassie's nose crinkle with their pungent aroma.

Dinner was a long affair, with everyone chattering on about gardens and painting, school and other everyday topics. They had found a nice rhythm with their get-togethers. After dinner, Cassie helped Baron clear the table and then they were shooed into the living room while tea was made. Within minutes, a plate piled high with oatmeal raisin and oatmeal chocolate chip cookies with walnuts appeared in front of them.

"Do you think we're spoiled?" Cassie asked, reaching for the first of several cookies.

"Spoiled? Us?" Bare grinned. "Naw, they're just fattening us up for the long voyage of winter."

"I can't eat another bite," Cassie finally exclaimed after reaching for, but not taking, a third cookie.

"We eat a lot for dinner here," Baron said, taking another cookie and pouring himself some more tea. He leaned back into the soft couch noticing yet again, that the Grammsies would occasionally look at each other, then at him and Cassie, the air charged with something left unsaid. Bare patted his belly. "I should probably eat a bit less," he chuckled, breaking the cookie into two pieces, then methodically eating first one, then the other.

Cassie shrugged. "I've lost weight even though I've been eating more lately. My Gramma makes lots of vegetable dishes and whole grain this and that—and then there's all the teas she makes me drink. Blech!" She grimaced, reached for her tea, took a sip. "I guess my metabolism is all wonky, 'cause Gramma worries I'm too skinny." She looked down and noticed how her new jeans were getting baggier, and even though she was sitting down and had just eaten, they were loose on top, too.

"Well, it's time to go, sweetie," Grandmother Iliana finally said. "It's nearly 10:00 p.m., and tomorrow's a school day—plus Selene and I have a few errands to run after you both leave in the morning."

There was that look again, Bare noticed, and wondered what sort of errands they were going to be on. Maybe it was a surprise of some kind, and he was just worrying too much about nothing. Still. . .despite the idyllic last few months, Baron couldn't ignore the undertow tugging at his thoughts and feelings, as well as his dreams.

Chapter 8

It was late Monday afternoon, and Baron had just left Cassie's so she could take a shower and get ready for the gallery opening. It was supposed to start around 8p.m., so there was still loads of time. They'd been working on their portfolios at Cassie's for a change while their Grammsies were out running their errands.

"Grams—I'm home!" Baron called out as he walked through the front door. He didn't sense her anywhere in the house, but just to make sure, he checked the den, the laundry room, his room, the kitchen, and even knocked on her closed bedroom door.

Maybe she's out back in the garden?

No.

Strange. She should have been back by now. He waited for a few moments, knocked again. "Grams—you taking a nap or something?"

Still no answer.

Oh that was brilliant, he realized. If she had been asleep, he'd just succeeding in waking her up. Grams had seemed a bit tired lately, and even though he knew she must be at least fifty, she still had the energy of a thirty-year-old.

When there still was no response, Baron cautiously opened her door.

"Grams—you in here?"

The bed was made—and she was definitely not in it. He wasn't worried, but he'd already checked the kitchen message board and there hadn't been a note. He went back into the kitchen to see if he'd missed something.

His note was still there: "Went to Cassie's to work on portfolios. Don't forget we're going to that art thing tonight at Star Gazers. We won't be that late."

Maybe she was at the grocery store—or the library. Grams just loved libraries.

He unhooked the cell phone from his belt, started to call Cassie, then changed his mind. She was probably in the shower, and the Grammsies were just fine.

Still. . .even though it had been a long time since he'd tried to crawl around in her mind like she so often did with him, Baron closed his eyes, reached out for her.

Nothing.

He wasn't that worried about not sensing her. It had been a long time since he'd tried to do it on purpose. Why had he stopped in the first place? They'd done it all the time when he was little, but then she had backed off, said something about allowing him his privacy now that he was growing up, becoming a man. How long ago had that been? Five years? Four? They only occasionally "played the game" as he used to call it. A telepathic hide-and-seek when he was little, then as he grew older, more of a checking in to say, "hey", and remind each other of things to pick up at the store and other everyday activities. Occasionally, though, he knew his Grams moved quickly through his mind, like a sudden wind, to see if he was okay, and occasionally to soothe him when he'd had a nightmare.

Baron finally decided just to call Cassie. She picked up on the first ring.

"Hello?"

"Hey, Cassie."

"I can hardly wait for the opening. Are you ready?"

"Yeah, me, too. I've been home awhile and Grams isn't back yet. Is she over there?"

"No—and no note, either. They're probably at the store or something. I know they had a lot of errands to run. It's not like we're little kids who need checking up on."

"Yeah. And it's not like they can't take care of themselves. I just feel kind of apprehensive, though. It's not like my Grams to be paranoid or anything, but she's always talking about this law firm I'm supposed to call if anything happens to her."

"So does my Gramma. She made me promise to not ever call the police, too. Weird, isn't it? You think we're all in the Witness Protection Program or something?"

"That's what I've wondered. How many times have you moved over the last few years again?"

This topic of conversation never seemed to bore either of them, and even though they'd volley the same questions back-and-forth time and again, Bare and Cassie hoped to uncover something they missed. They'd almost talked to their grandmothers about it, but the timing never seemed to be right. They both agreed that this subject might not go over so well.

"Within the same state or across states?"

"Both."

Cassie paused for a few moments to count on her fingers, whispering the places to herself. "Let's see—in just the past five years, I'd say about eight or nine—maybe even ten counting San

Diego. There was this little island off Puget Sound. Whidby, was it? Or Vashon. Then Tacoma, Washington, for a bit. Then there was this little town on the coast by Portland, Oregon—I forget the name. Then someplace in New Mexico—Taos! Then somewhere else in New Mexico. Oh, then we were in Texas for awhile. Oh—it was Las Cruces in New Mexico—how many's that?"

"I lost count—but Cassie?"

"Yeah?"

Baron paused, not believing his ears. "I bet I can tell you where else—"

"Oh yeah? Are you psychic or something?"

Baron could hear the smile in her voice. He already felt less stressed. Cassie seemed to have that effect on him. "Or something," he said, then added, "Truth-or-Consequences, New Mexico, and then you almost moved to Hawaii, but went to Idyllwild instead for a month or so, and then you came here, to San Diego."

"Cassie—you there? Cassie?"

"I'm stunned," she whispered. We've lived in all the same places at the same time. But we only stayed in Idyllwild for a week or so. We didn't actually live there."

"We were in Idyllwild for several weeks. So, it looks like we've definitely lived in the same places. Like one of us leaves first, then the other follows or something like that."

"Well that does explain a lot, then, doesn't it? Hey—" Cassie walked toward the front window when she heard someone outside the open window. "Gramma—I'm home—did you forget your keys?"

No response.

"Hey—hold on, Bare. There's someone outside. I think it's my Gramma, but I'm not sure."

She walked toward the front door, listened. Whoever it was pushed through the night blooming jasmine bush in an attempt to peer through the window. "Gramma—you're scaring me. Did you forget your keys?"

The window was open, and the curtains, despite their weight, ruffled in the evening breeze. All Cassie could see without going any closer or pulling the curtains back, was a vague form—and it wasn't her grandmother! An intense wave of nausea nearly doubled her over. "Bare—Bare—there's someone outside and I don't feel so good."

"I'll be over asap—don't open that door to anyone but me or our Grammsies!"

"Okay—hurry. I'm freaking here." Cassie leaned up against the wall, took a deep breath, then another and another before she looked toward the window again.

Whoever was outside had begun to back away from the window. Jostling the bush caused the night blooming jasmine to release its scent into the room. Cassie focused on the scent, rather than her rapidly beating heart, as she craned her ears to hear what they were doing.

Come on, Bare! Hurry!

The trespasser took a few steps onto the porch, paused, then turned toward the side yard. Cassie inched closer to the window, pulled back the curtain to close and lock the window. She saw their profile! Even hidden by the shadows cast by the half-moon's light, Cassie's first thought was Ms. Brunhof.

Chapter 9

When Baron arrived about ten minutes later, he gave Cassie a big hug before he walked through the entire house to make sure all the doors and windows were closed and locked. Fortunately, it had cooled down from earlier in the day, and the surprise Santa Ana seemed to be finally passing through.

Cassie followed Baron around the house, watching as he secured all the windows and doors, the phone clenched in her hands. "It was dark—but I swear it was Ms. Brunhof."

"If it was, she'd knock on the door, wouldn't she? No, it had to be someone else. Ms. Brunhof may be many things, but she's not that creepy."

"I know, " Cassie agreed, " but maybe she was just checking to see if I was home, or she wasn't sure if she should stop by unannounced. It sort of looked like her. Maybe I just wanted it to be her 'cause I knew it wasn't Gramma—" She paused, turned toward the kitchen door. "—and the alternative would be. . ."

"Let's not even worry about it. It was probably someone who had the wrong address or something."

"Yeah, but why didn't they answer when I called out? That's totally weird, isn't it? Maybe they couldn't hear me. I swear whoever it was made me nauseas. I can't even begin to describe the scent. At first, it was masked by the night blooming jasmine, but when they stepped onto the porch, it was so strong I was practically doubled-over ready to hurl, but then it passed when they left."

"Weird—but then so are you." Baron cracked a smile at her, pretended to duck an imagined punch.

Cassie giggled. "Yeah, that I am. I haven't eaten much today, either."

Baron shook his head at her, mimicking his Grams. "I'll make us something. What about that gallery thing? Still want to go?"

Cassie shrugged, plopped down in one of the cushioned chairs. "Yeah, but not right now. Can we hang out for a bit? I'd really like to make sure our Grammas are okay before we leave."

Baron furrowed his eyebrows, set his phone on the yellow-tiled counter. "She's still not answering—and it's after 9:00. This isn't like Grams."

"Mine, neither. She's like over-protective. Major overprotective—and hyper-responsible about staying-in-touch. She's never been out this late without calling me."

Baron paced around Cassie's kitchen, opening and closing cupboards, drawers. "Maybe it's 'cause they know we hang out all the time, that we have each other now, too."

"Would you stop that! You're making me dizzy."

"I always do this when I'm nervous or trying to work something out in my head. Something's been gnawing at me."

"What?"

"Well, remember our Grammas both said to contact their attorneys if something happened?"

"Yeah?"

"Well, I'm pretty sure something's happened to them. Let's call."

Cassie went to the bulletin board in the kitchen, removed a card with a standard business font that read: DAR & Associates. She handed it to Baron. "Does this look familiar to you?"

He nodded, reached for his phone on the kitchen counter, and was just about to push #1 on his speed dial, when they heard two sets of footsteps coming up the stone walkway, then on to the wooden porch. Both Cassie and Baron inhaled, held their breath, then exhaled with relief as a key was inserted into the lock and the door opened. They practically ran to the front door, feeling more like little kids than the nearly nineteen-year-olds they both were.

"Where were you?" Baron and Cassie cried out in eerie unison, wrapping their arms around their grandmothers and clinging like two-year-olds.

Iliana and Selene exchanged worried glances, chuckled. "Time just got away from us," Iliana said. Selene nodded, rested a hand on Baron's, then Cassie's, cheek. "I told you we should have called," she mock scolded Iliana, who made her way into the kitchen with the grocery bags. She called out, "It's not that they're little kids, but you're right. . .we're both usually home in the evening with them—how about some of my special cocoa with extra cinnamon and nutmeg?"

"And toast, too, please Gramma," Cassie called back. Her stomach was gnawing at itself again, the strange bout of nausea forgotten with the presence of her grandmother. What would she ever do without her? Cassie wondered, and her grandmother turned around, smiled, her eyes glistening with what looked like unshed tears.

Cassie knew her grandmother's cocoa would probably have

something else in it, too. She'd noticed how Gramma Iliana looked into her eyes for tell-tale signs, nodded, as if she could diagnose her ills with a mere glance—which she always seemed to be able to do.

"We bought some of that jam you both like—wild cherry," Iliana said, waving the jar in front of them. "Oh—what about that gallery opening?" She paused, made eye contact with Selene, then turned around to face the kids.

"We can check it out tomorrow. I don't feel like going out anymore."

"Me, neither," said Baron, practically tripping Cassie to get to his Grams to give her another huge hug.

"Into the living room with you both!" Selene yelled, trying to sound stern. "You're underfoot. Give us some room—or no snacks."

Even though the remainder of the evening was filled with animated chatter about all the errands they'd run, both Baron and Cassie sensed that they'd left out a good chunk of their day. There weren't enough bags to warrant so many hours, and they were all from Whole Foods.

Both Cassie and Baron were reluctant to question their grandmothers' whereabouts, as even though they were all adults, more or less, it didn't seem right. Both of them also tried, but failed, to find the right moment to tell the them about the stranger outside, or even begin to raise the issue of how they lived in the same towns—practically traveled together—but were never intertwined in each others lives until now.

What had changed to make it okay? Had they had a falling out and were finally mending bridges? It really did feel like an "all-of-a-sudden" to be hanging out like they were one big happy family. It just didn't make sense. Not that they were complaining, as truth be told, both Baron and Cassie hadn't seen their grandmothers both so happy and miserable at the same time, their eyes shifting from cloudy gray to bright blue, signaling their moods. At one time, Cassie even noticed that one of her grandmother's eyes seemed to be blue, the other gray, at the same time. She'd never noticed that before. What was that about?

She and Baron had been playing around with the time periods they lived in the same cities. While they almost always overlapped, at times, they were staggered, as if one moved, then the other waited, followed in a matter of weeks, or at the most, a month or two.

Coincidence? No such thing. Besides, neither of their grandmothers worked. They had their hobbies, like painting and gardening, but kept to themselves. . .raising their grandchildren, spending time with them. They had never really questioned this existence before. They'd been happy. No reason to worry. So why this feeling of foreboding?

Baron knew his Grams didn't need to work because of insurance money or an inheritance of some kind, but he'd never asked her about it. Why? He wondered if Cassie's Gram also lived off insurance, or if she worked.

He asked her later, just before he left.

"She always said it was an inheritance . . ."She paused to pick at a purple thread on her sweater, one of the many that her Grandmother Iliana had knitted for her. She balled up the threads and stuck them in her jeans' pocket.

"There is serious strange going on here," was all Baron said.

Chapter 10

Even though it was late November, and the semester was winding down, Ms. Brunhof had another series of absences. There was a sign-in sheet taped outside the studio door, and Baron and Cassie both scrawled their names.

Cassie yawned. "I could use some coffee. Wanna go to Star Gazers? The show's still up, too."

"Sure, my treat," Baron yawned.

They walked to the parking lot, then drove to the café in semi-silence. It was almost 9 a.m. and still on the cool side, but warm weather, another Santa Ana, was predicted for San Diego. Baron loathed Santa Ana winds almost as much as Cassie did. They made his skin crawl, and he was always wiping away imaginary insects. He much preferred the rain—even thunder and lightning. It didn't frighten him in the least. There was something soothing about torrential rain, and he and Cassie both slept better during storms. Another item in their long list of "things in common" that they seemed to add to daily. Over the past few months, they had become more than just great friends. They felt like—and had become—family. Their Grandmothers had a large part in nurturing that special bond, one they were sure would continue to be nurtured over time.

Baron walked through the café's wrought iron gate, held it open for Cassie. All of the outdoor tables were empty, the red canvas umbrellas collapsed and drooping. Once inside, Baron looked around the café, wondering why he was feeling on-edge.

"Anything you want, Cass." Baron reached into his jeans' pocket for his wallet, counted out a few fives, laid them on the counter. The barista smiled at him, her dark berry lips shimmering in the ambient light. When had her glossy black hair grown out? Baron wondered, noticing how she looked even cuter with those pigtails, the tips dyed a deep scarlet.

Cassie shrugged. "Whatever. Maybe a black hole or an event horizon—I don't really care so long as it's fully-loaded."

"The usual, then," the barista said, casting her eyes sideways at Cassie. Baron occasionally wondered if the barista wanted to hook up with him, but since he'd met Cassie, all he wanted to do was spend time with her. He didn't feel ready for a girlfriend yet. Besides, what did he need a girlfriend for now that he had Cassie? Maybe he'd missed a window with the barista, but then she was probably just doing her job. His life had always been so simple, perhaps too much so, but with Cassie and her Grams in his life now, it was complex in a curious, but good, way.

Baron nodded, smiled at the barista, realized that he didn't even know her name. He wanted to ask, but what came out of his mouth was, "Two of them, and one of those fruit bars, two of those chocolate chip cookies with nuts—please." He grinned again, and she smiled back at him, a huge smile that lit up her entire face. Even her eyes crinkled with delight. When her face relaxed again, and they looked into each others eyes for a moment, he noticed how even though they were almost obsidian, they had a deep sapphire tint around the edges, with little flecks of moonlight embedded in her dark sky eyes.

This exchange went unnoticed by Cassie who was looking around for a spot to sit. Even though they'd been here together dozens of times, she rarely noticed the layout, or the décor, as they were usually still trying to wake up, or exhausted after a long day. They tended to just focus on each other, their drinks, and their portfolios. Since the semester would be over in a few weeks, it was a good thing that they'd dedicated so much of their time together on their portfolios. Both of them were also glad they'd only enrolled in the one class, as it had been all-encompassing.

Cassie took a moment to look around. They'd taken down the art show, which was a shame. She regretted that they hadn't really checked it out when it was up, always thinking they'd have another chunk of time to do so. There'd been this one multi-media piece that Cassie had been totally fixated on. Baron had said it was too dark for his tastes, and didn't seem to like it much, but when Cassie had looked at it, she saw something moving behind the layers of oil pastel and ink, something glistening within the torn and shredded paper collage section. Something had spoken to her—but what?

There were three rooms, each with their own loose theme. One section had blood-red walls with wrought iron sconces. Another had old stuffed couches and chairs; a table here and there held local zines, newspapers. There was a man over by the magazine rack, flipping through some local rags. Cassie recognized him as the same guy they'd seen a few months before. He wasn't wearing that bulky black leather jacket this time, but she was sure that it was him.

The man seemed to stiffen a bit as his eyes followed a couple who walked past Cassie, arm-in-arm. He relaxed after they passed by, then walked outside to the front patio, sat down. Cassie thought his boots were pretty cool, like nothing she'd seen before. Was that leather? Or maybe they were made out of that new Vegan material that looked like leather but seemed to conform to a person's feet even better. Like calf-high moccasins, she mused, and caught herself just before asking him where he bought them. He was wearing jeans and a dark-blue T-shirt, and over that, a bulky jacket that looked like he was on his way to go camping, what with all the pockets and flaps.

Cassie returned to hover around Baron until the order was ready, then they both walked out to the front patio, past the man they both referred to as "leather-jacket guy". Cassie noticed him slip a hand into an inside pocket, grasp something rigid. His hand never left the pocket while he scanned the area in front of the café and across the street, turning only slightly in his chair to look left and then right.

"Does leather-jacket guy have a gun?" Cassie whispered, nodding her head back toward the man. "Do you think he's a cop or something? Maybe something's about to go down here. Let's get it to-go. My skin is tingling, and not in a good way."

Baron looked around, but didn't see anything out-of-place. An old beat-up green Volkswagen was parked just out front. Two middle-aged men in jogging suits were walking pit bull puppies. Leather-jacket guy stood up, leaned against the wrought-iron fence.

Baron shrugged. "Maybe. I think he's okay, though. I wouldn't worry. Here—have a bite of this one, too. It melts in your mouth."

"Ummm," Cassie murmured, allowing the butter cookie to dissolve on her tongue. "Hey! Isn't that—"She leaned forward in her chair, pointed just beyond the hedge to a figure rushing down the street. "Oh, never mind. I thought I saw Ms. Brunhof."

Baron chuckled. "You're seeing her everywhere these days," he said, remembering the incident a few weeks ago when Cassie swore it had been Ms. Brunhof lurking in her yard. "Maybe she's just ditching us. Even teachers need a break sometimes."

"Yeah—but still. She's been absent a lot, and when she's in class, she's there but not there. She doesn't look good, either. It's like she's aged twenty years over the semester or something."

"Really? I hadn't noticed. Maybe she's sick, has cancer or something."

"It's those headaches. Hers are worse than mine, I think."

"You're all heart, Cassie." Baron reached across the table to squeeze her shoulder.

"More like all stomach. I feel like eating now—" and she grabbed a gigantic brownie—or did they call them asteroid chews at The Star Gazer Café?

Chapter 11

Cassie and Baron hung out at the The Star Gazer for another hour or so, munching on cookies, sipping their coffees, not saying much of anything. They stopped paying attention to leather-jacket guy as they sketched a bit, doodled mostly. They heard a chair scrape, turned around. Leather-jacket guy was gone.

They stood up in unison, carried their dishes to the counter. "It's the right thing to do," Baron had said to Cassie one time, "as we're regulars, so it's like our place." Baron grinned at the barista, slipped a couple more dollars in the tip jar. She smiled, gestured toward Cassie with a tilt of her head, raised an eyebrow. Baron knew the barista was curious about Cassie, but for some reason, he didn't know quite how to introduce her, so he just smiled.

While he was holding the door open for Cassie, Baron turned around to look at the girl again. They locked eyes for just a moment or so, and Baron felt an energetic pulse in his chest. He'd never felt anything like it before, and even though it was just an unusual sensation, it was definitely a mixture of pleasure and pain. He turned away from her, lowered his head, smiled to himself, felt another energetic surge, and resisted the impulse to turn around to see if she was still looking at him,. He was certain she was. Not that he was full of himself, but lately, he'd noticed he knew things like Cassie did—like the guy in the café was okay, even though he never seemed relaxed, even when he was sitting totally still.

Cassie was a few steps ahead of Baron on the sidewalk. When Baron caught up with her, they resumed walking down the sidewalk toward Cassie's house. They were about half-way there when leather-jacket guy jacket appeared out of thin air, shoved Baron and Cassie into the bushes, then leapt out of the way, stumbling as if he lost his balance. Before the guy even hit the sidewalk, there was a crackling sound, a burst of green light, and he was gone.

As he was crashing into the bushes, Baron swore he'd seen something out of one of his nightmares: part human, part something else, skin hanging in clumps like an old lizard trying to molt. There were at least three of them, and they hissed at him, their eyes narrowed in obvious anger before leather-jacket guy had zapped them into a crackle of green light. The air stank, a pungent scent that clung to the insides of their nostrils like a ship dumping its bilge tank down at the harbor.

Instinctively, Baron pulled Cassie toward him, clenched her close. It was hard to breathe through the wave of vertigo as he vomited up his morning coffee and cookies. Cassie was moaning. Was he holding her too tight? Was she hurt? Knocked out and just now coming-to?

Baron wiped his mouth, and tried to avoid breathing through his nose, not wanting that stench to creep any further inside him. He heard Cassie vomit, the sound distant, as if it were filtered through water. She felt so far away from him, and yet there she was, by his side. If he didn't already know how much she meant to him, he realized it in full force now. If he had a sister, Baron would want her to be like Cassie.

The nausea began to pass, but his throat and eyes burned. To make matters worse, he could barely see anything in front of him, what with all those green spots ping-ponging around everything.

Baron clenched and unclenched his eyes, felt them tear, then tentatively opened them again, his field of vision was still hazy. The burning had subsided a bit, but his mouth tasted of metal and his skin tingled. Whatever that green spark was, it had made what hair he had on his arms stand on end. What would have happened if that burst had hit him, too? Or Cassie? What the hell was going on?

There was no question in his mind that they needed to get out of there—and now! What if those things came back? He clambered to his feet, pulled Cassie up off the ground, yelled, "RUN!" with such intensity that Cassie did as he commanded without hesitation. They cut across the neighbor's yard, up the side walkway, and into Cassie's back yard. Whatever that thing was, he hoped it didn't come back to follow them. He scanned the backyard, the bushes around the fence, and hoped that there weren't more lurking around the corner.

Baron pounded on the back door. "Gramma Iliana! It's us! Call the police—or those lawyer friends of yours—someone just got blasted!"

Chapter 12

When the back door opened, Baron and Cassie were startled to see a stranger. No! Two strangers, one towering over the man who opened the door. Large hands pulled them inside. Someone else closed and locked the door.

"What happened?" The man demanded. "Where is Verson?" Cassie and Baron, both still dazed, shook their heads, started to say something when two more men entered the room. "Did you see who shot at him? Anything?"

Still shaking and a bit winded, Baron studied the man in front of him. He was well over six feet tall. In fact, they were all well over six feet tall, which made Baron feel puny, even though he was nearly six feet and a bit on the pudgy side. They certainly looked official, if nothing else. He moistened his lips, focused on slowing his heart rate. *Calm down, man. Calm down.*

"Was Verson the guy in the leather jacket? We've noticed him around the café a lot lately. He kept looking around, left before we did—we were just walking home and he shoved us into the bushes—then poof!" Baron looked over at Cassie, who looked like she was going to hurl again.

"Poof? Could you be more specific?" The man asked, and if he was irritated at Baron's lack of response, he didn't show it. He seemed concerned. And rightly so, Baron realized.

"There was this green crackling light," Baron began. "Is he dead? What's going on? Where are our grandmothers? Who are you guys?"

The man who seemed to be in charge, who did all the talking, let out a heavy sigh, wove his fingers together, turned to the other three men, said, "Make arrangements. We leave tonight."

"If he hadn't pushed you two out of the way. . ."

"Now I feel like hurling again." Baron rested his head on the cool surface of the kitchen counter. Cassie just stood there, staring at this man who had taken control of her Grand-mother's kitchen.

One of the men walked back into the kitchen with some sort of i-phone or i-pod, tapping and sliding his fingers across the screen.

"I am Dar, the man there is T'ai, the others, Larno and D'Andri—they're taking care of the transport. We'll stop along the way."

"You still haven't told us what's going on—why we should even go with you! Where are our Grams? Who was after us? What's going on?"

"As I said, I am Dar. You have my card on your cold box, your refrigerator," he corrected himself. "It is clear that your guardians have not briefed you yet. Have not spoken about the protocol."

"Guardians? Briefed us? Protocol? I am so not getting what's going on here. Are we in the Witness Protection Program or something? What was that green flash thing? This is like one of those stupid TV thrillers or something. Where are our grandmothers?" Baron ranted on, waving his arms in the air. Cassie had never seen him so agitated.

"Or something," Cassie whispered, as a recent dream reeled into focus in her mind. Just the other night, she had **seen** these men. There had been a knock on the front door, and Baron had answered it. It was as if they'd all been waiting for them, as Baron had said, "That must be them. I'll get it." He'd then strode to the front door, taken a deep breath, opened the door for them.

Cassie had awakened, breathless with anticipation. Her heart pounding, her covers all tangled up—even more than usual. She often woke herself up from dreams where she was frightened or confused, but this one had seemed totally real. This wasn't how it had played out in the dream, though. Maybe the dream was the way it was supposed to have been, but something had gone wrong? She was certain she was awake and not asleep or unconscious on the sidewalk, so it could have been worse. Why hadn't she seen **that** unfold in her dreams? Cassie wondered what would have happened if she'd insisted they leave the café when she'd felt that first uncomfortable tingle. Her grandmother had always urged her to trust her feelings, her gift.

The same man who had knocked on that dream door, now extended his hand to Baron in real time. But what was real? She was having a difficult time defining it now, and wished she'd listened to her Gramma Iliana and written all her dreams down, no matter how innocuous they seemed. Yes, she definitely wished that she'd paid more attention to her dreams—especially the nasty ones. But this wasn't the first time a dream sequence had replayed itself, albeit somewhat altered, in her waking life.

"Verson was the person watching over you. We are your advisors. Your grandmothers' attorneys."

Baron looked from one man to the other, paused on the one named Larno.

"You're not like any attorneys I've ever seen," Baron remarked, trying not to stare. Even Dar, who seemed to be more mediator than muscle looked like he could do some damage.

Trying not to sound demanding, he asked, "Where are our grandmothers?"

Everyone turned toward the kitchen door as leather-jacket guy, or Verson, came in to the room.

Cassie gasped, pointed to him. "We thought you were dead! Thank you for pushing us out of the way—what were those things? Where did they go?"

He took a deep breath, exhaled, then with more calm than he felt, asked, "Why have you been watching us?"

Verson nodded to Cassie and Baron, approached Dar, held out what Baron had thought was an i-pod, but clearly wasn't.

"That was, as you say, a close call." Dar replied. "We need to take all precautions," he continued, then added, "for your protection, of course." He pressed his fingers together, tapped them, a gesture that Baron would notice him continuously repeat over the next few hours.

Dar, T'ai and Verson exchanged glances, said something in a foreign language that Baron recognized as the one his Grams spoke with Iliana. Dar's brows furrowed above dark, deep-set eyes as he tapped his fingers together. Then in English, he said, "We are sorry, but your Grandmothers seem to have gone on ahead. . .we are not sure as to their location yet. We probably will not know for some time as a security precaution."

Baron and Cassie exchanged worried glances. Then, for the first time, they locked minds. Their eyes widened when they realized what they had done.

Should we trust them?

Are they who they say they are?

They must be.

"When will you know that's what happened?" Baron looked askance at Cassie, then steeled his eyes on Dar and Version. "Since you're here, we believe you are who you say you are, otherwise we'd probably be dead right now. . ." Baron gestured toward the living room. "Please, make yourselves at home. Although I have the feeling you've been here before—and at my place, too."

"You are quite astute—which is to be expected. We apologize for any discomfort this may have caused you," Dar said, exchanging a glance with T'ai, who lead the way into the living room, continuing on through the foyer to stand at attention by the front door. Cassie plopped down on the sofa, thought about making tea for everyone, but she didn't feel like getting up. She didn't feel like doing anything but hugging the couch pillows.

Nothing for us. Thank you. Dar responded to her telepathically, then aloud, said, "Larno will remain in the cooking room, ah, kitchen, as a precaution." Dar nodded to Cassie, sat down in a chair next to the sofa. D'Andri and Verson waited until Dar motioned them to chairs. Baron noted all this, and was pretty sure Dar was the man in charge. So what did these other two do? They didn't appear to be guard-guards like the other two. Intel agents?

Cassie scooched into the sofa's corner, tried to resist the tears that were burning in her eyes. "Do you know where my Gramma is, where our Grammas are?" She wanted to, needed to, feel her grandmother's presence, both of their grandmother's presences, her mind twisted with anxiety. And what was with this "gone on ahead" business? She sniffed, reached for the tissue box on the coffee table, blew her nose. Her sinuses were still clogged up from that horrendous stench, and she half expected to have a headache, but thankfully didn't.

Dar exchanged glances with Verson again, leaned forward a bit in his chair. "How much did they tell you?"

"Not a thing—except to call you if something happened to them." Baron paused, tried to decide whether he should sit down next to Cassie or pull up a chair to the coffee table. He decided to keep standing.

Cassie curled into a ball, gave up fighting her tears. She wasn't used to crying, and she hated how constricted her throat became, how awful it felt. Then there was the throbbing sensation in her chest. "I'm sor-ry—but I'm just so wor-ried a-bout her. Everything's so weird— I need my Gramma!"

Baron sat down next to Cassie, put his arm around her. She leaned into him, began to relax. He was an anodyne. . .Her friend. Her Bare.

Dar stood up, walked to the window, pulled back the curtains, peered outside at the encroaching night. He scanned the sky, rested his eyes on a point in space, then closed the curtains.

"This is a difficult situation, as I am sure you are both aware. If only one of them was missing, I would not be as concerned. But both of them. Let us hope that they were together when intercepted. They are no doubt concerned about you as well. T'ai—"

"I've made a few inquiries. Nothing—yet." T'ai reached into his jacket pocket, pulled out his hand-held device, slid a finger across the screen, then tapped it several times. "Still nothing."

"Were there signs of struggle?" Vernon asked, his heavily accented voice having difficulty forming the words.

"Here? You've been here longer than we have—remember? Why did you come here in the first place?"

Dar ignored their question to ask another. "How do they leave messages for you if they are going to be gone?"

Baron turned to Cassie. "Usually Grams leaves a note—or a voice mail message—something—doesn't yours do the same?"

She nodded. "We know not to call the police. It was like our Grammas were already preparing us for something."

Baron looked from Dar to T'ai to Verson, then back again. "So what is really up here? I'm assuming our Grammsies contacted you. Otherwise, why would you be here now?" He took a breath, exhaled, then took another, trying to formulate his thoughts rather than barking out a barrage of questions.

"Who are you really? Federal agents or something? Why all this secrecy and stuff? If we're in the Witness Protection Program or something, don't you think that we have a right to know?"

"Yeah," Cassie said before blowing her nose again. She pulled her knees up to her chest, rested her chin on them. "Bare and me think we're in the Witness Protection Program. What else could be going on? We know that our families are connected somehow, but our grandmothers haven't said much, and—"

Dar interrupted Baron, waved his hand gently back-and-forth. "As to what is going on, that will take some time to explain. As to your guardians, I mean grandmothers, as we said, we believe they have gone on ahead. They would have left messages for you if they had the time." He looked around the room, frowned.

"But until we receive some sort of confirmation, it is just that. Can—I mean, may, we sit in the kitchen, at the table? It will make it easier to discuss all this if we are sitting together."

"What do you mean, 'gone on ahead' Where is ahead?" Bare asked for the third, or maybe fourth time. He'd lost count.

With arms crossed against his chest, Cassie realized that Baron had put on some weight since she first met him. He'd filled out, and looked menacing, which seemed so out-of-character for him. But unexpected circumstances like these often brought out qualities that didn't seem to fit.

"Please, let us sit," Dar said, standing behind one of the wood kitchen chairs. Once Cassie sat down, the others joined her at the long table, with Baron sitting next to her. Dar sat next to Baron, and once

T'ai and Verson joined them, the three attorneys—or whatever they were—laid their hands flat on the table. The one called D'Andri had gone outside, and Cassie seemed to relax a bit knowing that someone was standing guard—but against whom—or what? Were there more of those odd-looking creatures? She reached her tongue into the back of her mouth and she could still taste that gross scent that had permeated the air.

Baron wondered at their various gestures and how to interpret them. If he was sure of one thing, though, it was that they were stalling and had no intention to telling him or Cassie what was really going on.

Were they were all supposed to lay their hands on the table? Was it some sort of custom to signal serious matters were going to be discussed? Everyone sat still until their grandmothers' "friends" all placed their hands in their laps at once. Baron didn't think any of them looked like lawyers—but what were lawyers supposed to look like? Dar, maybe, with those dark blue slacks and jacket that resembled a suit, but the other four? They looked like hired muscle—or worse. He couldn't shake the feeling that maybe now was the time to start getting scared. He wanted to laugh, even tried to no avail, as his Grams was right. . .He did watch too many old movies—especially thrillers. They were like puzzles to him, puzzles he wanted to solve. It wouldn't help to let his imagination run rampant, as each minute that ticked by reminded him that they were knotted up in a big one. There had to be a simple explanation for this—for everything. He was going to listen respectfully. If their Grammsies trusted these men, then they did so for a reason.

And Cassie? She seemed to be totally tuned-out when she wasn't wrestling with the box of tissues. Baron wasn't used to hearing her cry, and it upset him more than he wanted to let on. One more aspect of their commingled lives that seemed off-kilter.

Dar finally began to speak. "I assume Iliana and Selene only told you a few details. No doubt this all seems strange, but I ask you to keep an open mind. Does the word, 'Mahrain', sound familiar to either of you?"

Without even looking at each other, Cassie and Baron shook their heads.

"What about the word, 'Haura'?"

The two nodded in unison.

"It's from a bedtime story my Gramma used to tell me—"

Baron interrupted Cassie—"The Waters of Nyr!"

The two teenagers looked at each other, incredulous.

"No way. The same bedtime story? This is getting weirder by the second," Baron said.

T'ai turned toward them, and his smooth face crinkled with an unexpected smile. "So that is how they kept Mahrain alive in you."

"What's Mahrain?" Cassie asked T'ai. Dar kept pressing and tapping his fingers together to the point that it was really beginning to annoy Baron, but something told him that it was best not to say anything.

"Tell me," Dar began, "have either of you noticed that you are capable of ah-hmmmm—T'ai—what is the word I am seeking here?"

T'ai closed his eyes for a moment, re-opened them. "Psychic phenomenon."

"Ah yes, psychic phenomenon."

Cassie and Baron nodded their heads in unison. "And I was wondering about making tea, and you were in my head saying something like 'none for us, thank you'.

"I suppose I did. It is so automatic for us I did not even think you did not communicate this way often."

"What about other unexplainable experiences?" Dar asked, then paused, watched as Cassie and Baron studied each other's faces for a moment, peered into each other's eyes.

"Well, I heard Grams speaking that same language you guys were. I'd never heard her speak it until just around the time Cassie and I started school this past fall. Now I know it was our Grammsies talking. They're from the same country or something. We know that much." He paused, studied his cuticles, fought the urge to bite them. "'The Waters of Nyr'—we—I—always thought that was just a bedtime story. But what's Mahrain?" He paused, rubbed at his eyes, added, "except for the dreams—"

"—and I have the dreams, too—and paint them!" Cassie added. "I get awful headaches, too. Horrible. Nightmares—oh, and I hurl a lot. Gramma makes me drink this gross tea."

"Hurl?" Dar looked perplexed.

"Vomit. Throw-up—"T'ai interjected.

"And my Grams can crawl around in my head. " Baron frowned. "I wish I could feel her in there now."

"Ah. Well, no doubt these are symptoms of life on Haura, our word for 'Earth'. The dreams, the images, these are imprinted in your minds. Tell me, do you sense other things?"

"Earth? Whaddya mean, Earth? As opposed to where?" Baron blurted out.

"Well, it looks like it has begun." Dar glanced over at Verson and T'ai, who was checking his gadget again. He shook his head. "I wish that your grandmothers had been able to explain more of this to you. No doubt they were planning to do so soon. Coming from them, it might be more, how do you say, T'ai, believable?"

T'ai nodded.

"So why are you here? How did you know we were being followed by those, those THINGS?"

"Verson warned us. We expected your guardians, your grandmothers, would be here as we had a meeting. When they did not answer the door, we let ourselves in." He reached into a jacket pocket, produced a key. "For emergency access."

It was getting dark, and the back porch light flickered on with a buzz. This caught Verson's attention, and he stood up, headed toward the back door.

"It's on a timer. The light," Baron said.

Verson still planned to investigate, and strode out the back door. He was gone for a few minutes before returning. Rather than sit down at the table, he closed the thin curtain covering the glass partition, then remained there, practically dwarfing the door.

"So what's going on?" Baron leaned forward, tried not to let his mounting anger and frustration show. They were here to help—but help with what? Monsters out of dreamtime?

"For your mutual protection, Baron and Cassie. For your safety." Dar glanced at T'ai again, who shook his head. "Verson—will you please scan the proximity again? We cannot be too safe here. Contact D'Andri. Determine if he has any more information. He will be bringing the other van around shortly."

Verson left the room, and they barely heard him as he walked down the hall checking one room after another. It was amazing to Baron how a guy that large could be so graceful—and quiet—in his movements, making barely a sound. He looked down at his shoes—at all their visitors' shoes—and noticed that they were all of the same soft-soled type.

"I think I've seen one of those things before," Cassie volunteered. "Remember that night we were going to go to the art show at The Star Gazer but our Grammas were late, and we were all worried and didn't go?"

"Yeah," Baron replied. "But you thought it looked like Ms. Brunhof. . ."

While Baron hadn't seen what—or who—Cassie had seen that night, he still shuddered at the memory of what he'd seen earlier. He closed his eyes, looked inside his mind. "I can draw it for you."

"That will not be necessary. We know what that thing, as you refer to it, is. There may be more of them in the vicinity, even more arriving shortly. That is why we need to leave tonight."

"There's more of them?" Cassie yelled, and Verson was in the kitchen before Cassie's voice trailed off.

"I knew there were more," Baron mumbled to himself. He turned to study Verson, realized that the guy could probably take the door off by its hinges if need be, and this gave him a brush of relief. If Verson's size alone wasn't enough, he'd outwitted that thing once, so he could do it again. Still. . .

"So what is it?" Baron paused, shoved his hands in his pockets, balled his fists, ripped through the pockets in his favorite blue corduroy pants. "That thing."

Dar continued to tap his fingers together. "We will get to that. For now, all you need to know is that our scans show they have not been detected in the immediate area. They are, as you surmised, not human, but may appear so with the means of what we call a synthsuit. They are not able to wear them comfortably for long periods of time, however, so unless an entire contingent arrives, we are safe for the moment."

Ms. Brunhof flashed into Baron's mind, and he remembered how her skin appeared the last time she'd been in class. A synthsuit? What was that?

"Cassie—maybe you're right. Ms. Brunhof could be one of them," Baron said, turning toward her, reaching for and grabbing her hand. She clasped her other one around his, and Baron could feel it shaking.

Her jaw dropped. "No way. I mean I thought it looked like her—but it was dark. She's been so awesome to me, to us. How could she want to hurt us?" Cassie continued shaking her head back-and-forth, not willing to believe that it was even possible.

"Tell us about this Ms. Brunhof," Dar said. "Does she know where you live?"

"I dunno. She's our studio arts teacher," they said in unison.

Dar nodded, turned to Verson, raised an eyebrow. Cassie and Baron didn't know how to interpret the expression, but both felt something significant pass between the two men.

"Yes, it is not unusual for them to—how do you say, live among you? They are shrewd in general, and many of them can mimic human behavior without much effort. It is possible that she is one. We know that there are several living here in San Diego, as we have intercepted their signals." Dar paused, gestured to the door leading into the living room. “Perhaps you should pack a few things, Cassie. Just essentials. We will be leaving shortly.”

He turned to Baron. “We will send someone with you to your home. Verson—“

Baron shrugged, said, “I don’t really need anything. Where are we going anyway?”

“To our downtown office. We will be safe there until we leave," Dar replied.

Baron grabbed Cassie's hand, said, "Where are you taking us?"

Dar understood that he would need to tell Baron something. The last thing he wanted was to take the two against their will. “We are going on a little trip to what you may call a safe house.”

Chapter 13

It was way past dark when D'Andri returned to Cassie's house with three more buffed-out men. Baron was amazed at how Cassie's house had become Alien SWAT Central, and wondered how many of these guys lived here in San Diego or were hovering over earth, waiting for action, in some Mother Ship.

All D'Andri said by way of introduction was, "These are our escorts," as the three men entered the kitchen and stood at attention. They were all massive, like Verson, Cassie noticed, trying not to stare as she trailed her eyes from toe-to-head after pushing herself from the kitchen table to put the kettle back on.

"That will not be necessary," Dar said. "We will be leaving shortly."

Cassie nodded, looked to Baron for support. "We're all packed," Baron said, gesturing to the three duffle bags and large portfolio holding their combined artwork. He felt they should have packed something for the Grammsies, even though Dar had indicated earlier that it wouldn't be necessary.

"So I see," said one of the escorts, Nal. He wasn't used to this constant small talk, this stating of the obvious, that seemed to be so prevalent among Haurans. Perhaps it was his training, or just his natural proclivity to conserve mental, as well as physical, energy until it was really needed.

Baron noticed that Nal bore a striking resemblance to Verson and T'ai, in that they were all exceptionally tall, large-boned, and buffed-out. When had Verson and T'ai changed into those dark green suits? The fabric seemed to be painted onto their bodies; the suits clung that tight. He stifled an inappropriate chuckle. They were all wearing those dark shades, too, and they reminded him of a SWAT team from some low-budget SciFi flick rather than military or whatever they were. "Escorts" was probably some loose translation for "guards" or "police squad".

Since Dar seemed visibly relieved at their arrival, Baron experienced a few moments of clarity. They really were in imminent danger, and Dar really did care about their safety. Dar didn't bother with formal introductions this time, either. The feeling of danger was further heightened by their hushed speech interspersed with gadget checking.

Baron strained to hear what they were saying, realized that it was yet a different language than the one spoken by his Grams. Am I going to have to learn all these new languages, too, he wondered, feeling momentarily overwhelmed at the prospect until the three men picked up Cassie's and his bags, and T'ai gestured to them to follow.

Cassie turned around to glance at the familiar surroundings of home one last time before they walked out the door. In the way that she often knew things, she was certain they wouldn't be back for a long, long time—if at all. What would happen to their house? To all the stuff they had to leave behind? She wanted to press the pale yellow walls into her memory, along with the comfy old brown sofa where she had spent countless hours reading, drawing, and talking to her Grandmother. Who would water the plants in their absence? Cassie almost turned around to make sure they weren't too dry. Her Grandmother had taught her to check the soil for moisture time and time again, but she always seemed to under-water them. Her Grandmother would "tsk-tsk" at this, and get a faraway look in her eyes.

After taking one last look at the room, Cassie allowed herself to be gently ushered through the door, down the walkway to the large dark van where Baron was already waiting, leaning again the front hood.

There was an odd arrangement of seats in the back of the van, obviously modified from the original. One of the "escorts" sat in the back, his bulk seeming to occupy the entire back seat. Cassie and Baron sat in the middle, and then the other two escorts took their positions on either side, leaving an empty seat for Dar, they assumed. It remained empty, though, as T'ai sat in the driver's seat and Dar climbed in beside him.

When the doors slammed shut, Cassie winced, and Baron took her hands in his, squeezed. "It's going to be okay, Cassie. It's really going to be okay."

"I wish I felt something—anything. All I want to do is curl up into a little ball and go to sleep." She leaned against Baron as the van began to back down the driveway. The two escorts met each others gaze, and Baron wished that he knew what all these expressions meant. Were these two trustworthy? What if this were all a set-up, and nothing was as it seemed?

* * *

T'ai drove cautiously through the residential area toward the downtown Gas Lamp area, careful, despite their haste, to obey all the usual road signs. The last thing they needed was to have to deal with the police pulling them over and searching the van. Not that it would ever get that far, though, as if the police were to pull them over, they would need to resort to special measures—and T'ai didn't want to cause any harm to the innocent.

Once they were out of downtown, and on the freeway, he relaxed, changing lanes only as often as was necessary, until he took the exit which lead to their office building just outside of Old Town.

A new moon was in the night sky, and there was just the barest sprinkling of stars. The temperature had dropped down into the 50s, but thankfully, it was a clear night. T'ai pulled into the unattended parking lot, drove around to the back of the building that led to the service entrance, where the freight elevator was located. Once the van stopped, Larno, who had been sitting behind Cassie and Baron, opened the back of the van. He climbed out with greater agility than Baron would have thought possible in a man of his size.

Baron hadn't noticed any weapons on any of the men, and wondered what all those gadgets they carried could do. They would have to have some sort of weapons, would they? The tension was real and palpable. He felt surges of adrenalin coursing through his body, and even though he didn't want to have to run for his life, he knew that he was amped-up enough to do so.

But could Cassie? It wasn't that he thought she was weak or not physically fit, but there had always been a frailness to her—and it wasn't just the headaches that caused him to feel this way. He sensed the truth of it, and this insight disturbed him. She was part of his life now, and the possibility of her being torn away from him was gnawing at his thoughts.

Another man approached the van and exchanged a few words with T'ai. He made a hand gesture that they both inter-preted as meaning to wait. It was quiet, but the telltale sound of electric wires hummed nearby, mingled with the sound of an elevator whirring up its shaft. There were a variety of buildings that reminded him of warehouses—not office buildings.

Where are we going? Cassie asked Baron, and for the second time today, their minds were linked. If she wasn't so stressed-out and worried, she would think it was cool they could talk like this.

Probably down beneath street level, Baron responded.

Larno returned from his rounds, nodded to Dar and T'ai. "Come—we go now," Dar said.

The guards, or escorts, as they'd been introduced, scanned the perimeter on foot and with their hand-held devices until they reached a freight elevator. Once inside, Dar slid a key into a locked panel that moved to the side revealing a control panel. Baron thought it was odd there weren't any numbers or visible symbols to indicate levels or floors. How did this elevator function? Where were they going?

Within moments, the keypad, for want of a better term, began to emit a pale umber glow. Baron watched as Dar passed his hand over it. The color changed to a dark rust, almost orange, and the air quality in the elevator seemed to thin a bit, the temperature to rise.

"We will be leaving shortly," Dar said, attempting a smile. "You will feel a bit lightheaded, perhaps a bit disoriented—and you, Cassie, please try not to hurl, as you say it."

Cassie looked around for something to hold onto, but there wasn't anything, so she reached out to Baron, who put his arms around her, drew her close against him. Being a protector was a new experience for him, and even though it gave him purpose, he loathed the need for it.

Dar passed his hand over the panel again, and the color panel changed to another hue. Even the air quality seemed moister, thicker, like they were in a sauna or a steam room. After Dar made one more pass over the panel, Baron reeled at the odd sensations inside his body. He gripped Cassie tighter, closed his eyes. In that moment, there was a lurch, as if his insides were trying to escape like sweat through pores. The moment seemed to expand in all directions, as did the strange tugging sensations inside his body.

And then it was over, and there was Dar smiling, T'ai looking relieved, and three of the guards standing at attention. Cassie, amazingly enough, wasn't hurling, but seemed as if the weight of the last few days was gone from her eyes.

The lift door opened, and a woman's voice called out. "Welcome aboard, as you Haurans say."

Cassie and Baron turned toward the source of this new, yet strangely familiar, voice. There, right in front of them, was the barista from the Star Gazer!

"No way!" Baron yelled, wanting to reach out to hug her. She moistened her rich berry lips, smiling. "I couldn't say anything to you two until I knew you knew."

"Figures," Cassie muttered. "So much for that six degrees of separation stuff. It's more like zero."

"Don't tell me you're our pilot," Baron chuckled. "Oh—did you bring any drinks—or cookies—with you?" he asked, noticing that his stomach was rumbling just at the sight of her.

"No, I'm just along for the ride home. My name's Ooli, by the way. There's no reason for me to stay on Haura any longer—now that you two are headed toward your destiny."

Cassie felt one of her telltale chills, shuddered, and turned toward Baron. The look that passed between them was clear. . .They had at least ten-thousand questions—and more were being added to the list. When would they get some real answers?

Chapter 14

The starslip rose vertically through the underground chamber until it reached street level. Camouflaged in part by an artificial fog bank, it rose into the sky, clearing the building. It hovered for a few moments before rising up and through the protective covering of a patch of dark storm clouds. It zip-zagged between several layers of clouds before leaving Earth's—or Haura's—atmosphere.

Everyone aboard the starslip visibly relaxed. Baron wondered for a moment if they were worried about getting fired at. It was San Diego, and there was a major airport and a military presence. Did the starslip show up on their radar? He decided to brush that negative thought away, and allowed himself to relax a bit while he looked through the transparent horizontal ovals that functioned like windows. He and Cassie were in a space ship. A frigging space ship, and kept mentally pinching themselves to make sure they weren't dreaming.

Now well above earth, Baron peered into an inky blackness. What an awesome canvas, he thought, and made a mental note to try it out for a future art project. Maybe it was because as an artist, he could see, sense, and feel nuances of color. Sometimes, he swore he could hear colors, too. The word for it was just on he tip of his mind. Synesthesia. Or perhaps it was because his dreams had been filled with these skies as well as others more alien.

None of that really mattered now that he and Cassie were miles above Earth and separated from empty space by a few inches of material that seemed too porous to protect them from the elements. The starship's surface was smooth and yielded slightly when he touched it. What sort of metal did that?

Cassie was nodding pensively, her mind working in another realm, checking these images against her dreams.

We're on our way! She exclaimed inside her mind and Baron's. He nodded as well, which elicited a rare smile from Dar.

"Now that you are no longer on Haura, your abilities should grow stronger. The closer you get to your home, and your family, the stronger will your abilities be."

Cassie and Baron turned around to greet Dar, who had been aft—if there was indeed an aft in this transport vessel—attending to the details of their departure and ensuing arrival—to where, they still didn't know.

"I can't help wondering what our Grammsies would say to us now. I wish they were here." Baron reached out instinctively for Cassie's hand as they continued to stare out the port window at trails of multicolored and faceted light. It's probably some sort of force field, Baron thought, chuckling at how his Grams would say he watched too much TV. He wished he knew more about astronomy. And here he was on a journey to an alien universe, where nothing would look the same in the night sky.

"Yeah. I feel they're okay. Isn't this cool, though? Despite everything. This is way cool."

Cassie nodded, gripped Baron's hand tighter.

"Enough sightseeing for the moment. It is time to how do you say, buckle down? Dar led them down a short corridor into an area with a wall of horizontal luggage compartments embedded in squishy foam. "Please wait here for a few moments, and an attendant will assist you."

They waited for just a few moments before someone else appeared. He was dressed differently than the others. Some sort of loose clothing that looked like pajamas to Baron. The attendant didn't introduce himself, but seemed pleasant enough. He gestured them forward with a slight wave of a hand. Cassie and Baron followed the attendant past the storage section to a series of berths that looked like shower stalls.

Baron looked at Cassie, noticed that the corners of her mouth were turned down, sensed that she seemed wary. He understood wary, especially since this was all so new, so strange. Only their grandmothers would believe them if they wanted to tell someone.

But whom would they tell? It wasn't like they had a group of friends back on earth. There wouldn't be anyone who would notice they were gone, much less miss them. Everyone he cared about was either on this ship or listed as whereabouts unknown.

The attendant began the process of getting Cassie situated first. Just before the door sealed her in, she looked into Baron's eyes and he knew she was frightened. He leaned forward, pressed a kiss on her forehead. She beamed back at him, relieved.

"Nighty-night," Baron said, and Cassie closed her eyes.

The process was repeated with him, and Baron thought the chamber was pretty comfortable. He eased into the squishy foam, or whatever it was, sighed. *Totally comfy*, he said to Cassie, hoping she felt the same.

Cushioned in the stasis chamber, Baron could barely keep his eyes open. He attempted to stifle a series of yawns, then realized he couldn't move his hands or his arms. He wished that he could see Cassie, wondered if she was sleepy yet, and how long they were going to be asleep. Dar hadn't said how far away they were going. He'd been almost playful when divulging that they were going to take a short trip to a safe house. How did someone like Dar, who was from another galaxy entirely, define short anyway? Baron yawned again, eased toward sleep.

In the adjoining chamber, Cassie felt the effects of whatever they'd pumped into the stasis chamber almost immediately. She reached out for sleep as if it were her Grandmother's hand, and was looking forward to waking up on the other side. She held an image of Gramma Iliana sitting on a couch with a cup of tea, waiting for her. She sought her mind for the scent of the aromatic tea, then focused on adding Gramma Selene, then Bare, and herself. All reunited when they arrived. Once the image was complete, she sighed, willed herself to let-go, full knowing that the drug-filled stasis chamber would keep her asleep until they arrived.

Chapter 15

Cassie was startled awake. Someone was in the chamber with her! How could someone else be in here, she wondered, then realized she must be dreaming. She called out to Baron automatically, and he responded immediately.

Bare, there's someone else with us here. Look—

Baron refocused his eyes. *It's that guy from your drawings, isn't it?*

Hello Baron, Cassie. I'm Danyal. Looking forward to meeting you both once you arrive. Oh— he paused, looked askance at something just out of Cassie and Baron's view, *just in case no one has told you yet, I'm your older brother.*

Brother! Cassie and Baron thought in unison, and realized that they could see each other clearly as well.

Yes, brother, Danyal said, and it sounded as if he were there with them, as if they could almost touch the hands extended to them. Both Cassie and Baron felt an electric charge surge through their bodies as they were somehow transported into a chamber face-to-face with Danyal, who chuckled at their surprised expressions.

Cassie looked down at her pale slender hand grasped within Danyal's much larger and dark hand, then at his face, which was no longer hidden in the shadows of Cassie's mind or paintings, then back at their clasped hands. Danyal released Baron's hand, then Cassie's.

Brother? They repeated.

No doubt you have many questions—and we have a long trip ahead of us where I hope to answer them. What have the others told you?

Others? You mean Dar and the goon squad? Cassie and Baron looked at each other, shrugged.

Yes, and your surrogates—what have they told you?

Surrogates?

Yes, your surrogates. The ones who bore you on Haura.

We don't know what you're talking about. Our parents are dead, Baron said. *Our grandmothers raised us.*

Danyal shook his head, pressed his hands together just like Dar did before he spoke of serious matters. Part of Cassie's mind was focused on how strange this meeting was, how they'd managed to be transported to this unfamiliar room from inside the ship's stasis chambers. Another part of her mind was stunned at seeing this man from her painting in front of them. There was a sadness to his dark green eyes, which were small, wide-set, and slanted upward unlike any she had ever seen. They reminded her of a set of Slavic dolls she had once seen at a museum show. His skin was pale like hers, but there were dark circles under his eyes as if he'd been ill for a very long time, ill and in the kind of pain that prevented him from sleeping well. Then there was the part of her mind that was trying to wrap itself around what he had said. He was their brother. That meant she and Baron were brother and sister. How could that be? Were they twins? When was his birthday anyway? It was odd how they never spoke of birthdays.

How do we know you're really our brother? Baron said, giving Danyal a once over. The guy wasn't very tall, but he had the broad shoulders of a much larger man, the rest of his body on the thin side. He didn't look anything like Cassie or him, but he definitely looked like the guy in her painting.

Cassie and him. They were brother and sister? It made sense after all the weirdness—but why hadn't anyone told them before? What was going on?

Please. Sit. Danyal gestured to just behind where Cassie and Baron were standing, and a bench appeared. Neither of them had noticed it before. Where were they anyway?

They sat down, felt a hard surface, realized that they still had to be on the ship even though it didn't feel like it. The air was suffused with a cool mist and felt soothing—just like the Star Gazer Café, Cassie realized. There was a faint tinge to the mist as well. Was it blue? Green? Turquoise? The hue seemed to shift as it swirled around them like a wall of misters in a lush garden patio.

Your grandmothers, as you call them, were—are—your surrogate mothers. As embryos, you were each placed into their wombs, sent to Haura, where they gave birth to you. Where they protected you. Where they—

*Whoa, whoa, whoa—*Baron tried to stand up, but the bench clung to him as if he had become part of it, or it him. He looked at Cassie, amazed that she sat there so serenely. While her eyes were closed, they moved side-to-side beneath the lids, as if she was in the throes of a dream.

Where are they now? She asked without opening her eyes.

I don't know, but our biological mother—and father—and mine as well—are safe on one of our moons. I long to see their faces again before I die. Their names are Galana and Bahar. Do they sound familiar to you? These names are probably strange to your ears as you have been given Hauran names, but when we are all reunited again, there will be a naming ceremony, and you will receive your true Mahrainian names.

What! Cassie and Baron yelled out in unison. Danyal winced at the sound, rubbed his temple, sighed, the mist billowing around him, changing hue to a dark blue, then so dark that they could barely see.

What happened to the light? Cassie asked.

It is nearly night here now, and I am tired. It is difficult for me to sustain this contact, to keep you here. I've tried to reach you before—reach you both before—but was only able to walk a bit in your dreams, Cassie. Baron—

Yes?

Promise me that you won't say anything about our meeting. There may be spies aboard the starslip—and no one wants you imprisoned here with me more than them.

Imprisoned? Baron leaned as far forward as the bench would allow, tried to see Danyal's face through the darkening mist.

Yes, I have been imprisoned here for quite some time. That is why you were created, why the surrogates came forward. At first, our mother and father did not know of the advisors' plans to create you. As strange as it may sound, they did this to protect our family and its trust—and you as well. Danyal sighed again. *Our ways are complicated to you now, but you will learn. Your chance to exist would have been destroyed if they hadn't done this. The important thing is that you have survived, and that you are on your way home.*

Danyal paused for a few moments, closed his eyes. He seemed to be searching his thoughts. Baron could almost see him pressing his hands together, his fingers tapping, tapping, tapping, as if this simple gesture was like a drill burrowing deep within his mind to extract a core sample.

At last he spoke. *The Toori found you, didn't they? That's why you were taken from Haura, placed in stasis aboard the starslip.*

The Toori? You mean those ugly shape-shifting monster things? Baron felt his skin grow cold at their image morphing within his mind.

Danyal was quiet for a few moments, his image fading from their minds. He reappeared, fuzzy around the edges, like an old sepia photograph.

Yes, those are the Toori. They are loyal to our uncle, our father's brother. He is a complicated man. Greedy. No, that is not the word. I do not even know the word for what he is. Our parents are in exile because of him. I am imprisoned because of him—and since he learned of your existence, he wants to capture and imprison you as well—unless—

Unless what? Baron asked

Cassie, who had been unusually silent while Danyal spoke within the gloomy room, finally spoke.

We tell him how to find—and unleash—The Waters of Nyr, she whispered.

And then both Cassie and Baron felt an odd tugging, a magnetic pull, and they were wrenched from Danyal's and each other's presence, returned to their bodies in the stasis chambers, and into a deep dark sleep which would last the remainder of their journey to Mahrain's furthest moon, Poora.

Chapter 16

After several months traversing space, the starslip docked at a base known as PI, located on Mahrain third moon, Poora. The station usually had a minimal crew, but this had changed with the news of Dar's imminent arrival. Alerts had gone out that there had been a Toori attack back on Haura, so a thorough search of the area was conducted. The only sign of a Toori presence was an old Trilune cargo ship that had clearly been ransacked for parts; it was definitely grounded, and no longer fit for flight.

When the stasis timer on Baron and Cassie's pods released, Ooli had been awake for several days. She waited anxiously outside their adjoining chambers, carrying two containers of revitalizing tea. They sipped the brew without whining.

"This we know," Baron said, smacking his lips at the bitter taste.

"Does anything taste good from our world?" Cassie asked.

"Come on, " Ooli smiled, "you've had my ooey-gooey lemon bars—how can you ask that?" She grinned, and her eyes lingered on Baron for a few moments before she turned around, and led them toward the ship's exit.

"Wish I had one about now," Baron said, stifling a yawn. He expected to feel stiff from the trip, but as he stretched his limbs, he was relieved that he wasn't. Just how far had they traveled, he wondered, and how far were they away from Earth, or Haura? The Mahrainian word was still unfamiliar to his tongue.

Cassie expected to be vomiting up her tea any minute, but surprisingly, it stayed down. She ran her tongue over her teeth, relishing the tea's taste.

It didn't take long for the "visit" with Danyal to slam back into their conscious minds. Just in time, they remembered that he had asked them to keep their meeting a secret. Did this mean not to say anything to Dar, either? Dar and his attendants had to be trustworthy, as here they were all in one place, and it felt safe—or safer—now that they weren't trying to outrun the Poori or the Toori—whatever their names were. He shuddered for a moment. Who knew that Ms. Brunhof would turn out to be a shape-shifting monster!

What about Ooli? Could she be one, too—or one of the spies Danyal had mentioned? They looked at her, then back at each other. *No*! resounded firmly in their minds as they shook their heads in unison.

Ooli turned around, looked at them, curious.

"Just getting the bugs out."

"Yeah," Cassie grinned, agreeing. "The bugs."

"Ah yes," Ooli responded. "The ringing in your ears, I think you call it. That will pass. Take it easy, as you may experience some dizziness. We lovingly refer to it as the transport dizzy flu. Come with me. We'll get you all cleaned up before we get debriefed."

Cassie and Baron followed close behind Ooli, hoping that their unspoken fears didn't enter her conscious mind. Both focused on concern for their grandmothers to thwart any other thoughts from entering their minds.

As soon as they stepped off the starslip, Dar was there to meet them, his hands clasped together in greeting.

He nodded to them, said, "We are not without ceremony here in exile. Please to follow me. You may freshen up, as you say, before you meet your family, who are quite anxious to see you."

Cassie and Baron both perked up. "Family!" they called out in unison.

Dar pressed his fingers firmly together. "Yes, family. Would that it was your parents," he sighed. "That is one aspect of all this your guardians, I mean, your grandmothers did tell you that was somewhat true. An aunt and possibly some cousins. . ." his voice trailed off as they came to the end of the hallway.

Dar tapped his fingers together, and while he appeared to be resisting the urge to frown, Baron wasn't sure what the expression meant.

Then it hit him! Danyal had said his parents—their parents—were in exile. He looked at Cassie, wished that they hadn't made that promise to Danyal. But wouldn't Dar know?

Unless they were being lied to. . .But who was lying, Danyal or Dar?

"I will leave you now. These attendants will see to your needs." Dar nodded to them, then turned to walk down the hall. The two attendants who accompanied him slid open a panel to reveal what looked like a key pad, but pulsed with a wan blue light. After they each waved their hands over the pad, it emitted a pale green glow, and a door slid open to reveal a small room with cushioned stools and a low table.

Once the attendants left, Baron grabbed Cassie around the arms, bent down to whisper in her ear. "Danyal said our parents are in exile, not dead. Who do we believe?"

She closed her eyes, moistened her lips. She was thirsty. So thirsty, and was still having a difficulty time focusing her thoughts. "Do you think Dar is telling the truth?"

Baron shook his head, sighed, sat down on one of the stools. "I really don't know who to believe, but I do believe our Grammsies. They said our parents died in a horrible accident. Now I'm wondering if they were murdered. None of this makes sense. I don't even feel like I'm in my own body—much less light-years away from Earth."

Light-years away from Haura, they corrected themselves mentally.

"We're going to have to learn to speak Mahrainian," Cassie said. "So we understand what they're saying. I want to know what everyone is saying when they speak all those other languages. I counted at least three, maybe four."

Baron frowned. "It sounds like a difficult language." Then he grinned when a thought occurred to him. "Hey—maybe they have that *Rosetta Stone* program for Mahrainian." He meant it as a joke, trying to reconnect with his usual playful nature, then realized his lighter side had all but disappeared.

"Don't you feel that a part of you already knows it, though?" Cassie stared off to the left, recalling a bit of a dream where she was sure someone was speaking their native tongue—and that she had understood it. But there would be more than just their proverbial native tongue to learn.

One of the attendants came up behind them, laid a hand on Baron's shoulder, startling both of them. Baron whipped around in his chair, then realized who it was. He mumbled something under his breath, his body still shaking. The attendant gestured to what resembled a bathroom, then to an alcove where clothes were folded neatly on two shelves. He smiled, lowered his eyes, and bowed out of the room.

"You think he's from another planet? He doesn't look like Dar and the others."

"Like anyone here looks like them much. It's probably like Earth—I mean Haura—all types of people. Is that what they call them here?"

"Well, I don't think he speaks English. My head is swirling with all the different languages here. I wish we could go outside to see what Poora looks like, if it's one of the places I've been drawing or dreaming about. Aren't you curious?"

Baron was quiet for a few moments, shrugged. "I guess I care more about what's going on. Do you think the room is bugged, that we're being watched? Hasn't it occurred to you that maybe it's Danyal we shouldn't trust rather than everyone else? Just because he could get in our heads and drag us to wherever he was—is—without our bodies on, doesn't mean he's trustworthy. It just means he has some insane powers or something."

Cassie nodded. "I'm going to freshen up—hope they have running water here!"

While Cassie was in the bathroom, Baron explored the small suite of rooms they would be sharing. There was another sitting area with an ingenious table with extensions to make a larger one, sleeping palettes that reminded him of futons, and a closet alcove. No place to cook, and no evidence of food, so he supposed there was some sort of dining room or mess hall here.

But where was here exactly? The place was so without embellishment, purely functional, which caused him to think that this was a step up from a military barracks or something.

Baron.

He heard the voice far away in his mind, sifting up through his consciousness.

Baron.

There it was again, but he didn't recognize the sound of the voice.

Be careful, Baron.

Who was it? It was certainly not his Grams, and it didn't sound like Cassie. Could it be Ooli? The voice sounded androgynous. Could it be Danyal? Someone else trying to get his attention, to warn him? But of what?

Chapter 17

Refreshed, and now wearing the Mahrainian version of what he and Cassie had first thought were pajamas, they were ushered through a series of hallways by yet another attendant. This one seemed more like a bodyguard, though, as he was about the size of Verson and the others and wore that same skin-tight blue uniform. The suits were so tight, that Baron wondered how they breathed, much less were able to move so swiftly. Stealth. Yes, that's the word he was looking for: Stealth. Some sort of alien ninja assassins. He stifled a laugh, wondered at the chaos of his thoughts—like the past had slammed back into the present. It was a weird sensation. . .all these commingled thoughts, snatches of dreams, telepathic images, and scents. Baron wondered if Cassie was experiencing the same thing. He allowed his mind to drift toward hers, and she turned to him, her eyes wide and curious.

Just checking in to see if the comlink is still open.

Cassie smiled at him, counted her blessings as even though their life had been turned inside out, she had her Baron. Her Bare. He was here. Her friend, her brother. But why hadn't their grandmothers told them this? If it was true, they must have had good reasons to leave this information out.

There was a synchronous pause, as everyone seemed to be looking through the thick window at a vast desert landscape, where various sizes of boulders and slabs of rock cast a multi-layered collage of shadows. It was a sobering vision to both Cassie and Baron, who had recently left a lush landscape—perhaps for the rest of their lives. It reminded them of the desert, yet the stones were more varied in color. One in particular caught Cassie's eye. Purple. It was an intense shade of purple that reminded her of blueberries.

"No wonder Ms. Brunhof loved exotic plants," Baron whispered to Cassie.

"Do you think she was from here?"

"Or somewhere very like it," Baron replied.

"The Toori," Dar interrupted, "are from a more desolate moon than this. Psion IV, which is now a mining colony, was their home for generations. Poora has many sites of beauty—which I hope you will soon see—and this desert, as you call it, has its own beauty."

"We didn't mean to say it was ugly, Dar. Sorry," Cassie said, the heat crawling up from her chest to her face.

"We meant no disrespect," Baron added.

Dar tapped his fingers. "If things go according to plan, we will provide all-terrain suits for you and take a hike. The others will be here soon. Would you like some water? Tea? Are you hungry yet? You were fed nourishment during stasis, so you may not need to eat for some time."

Cassie and Baron said yes to the water, and a familiar attendant poured them each a tumbler full from a green stone carafe that Baron thought looked like jade. He wondered if it was a local stone.

"While we wait for the others—ah, here is Verson and T'ai. I am hoping they have word of your Guardians."

Both Verson and T'ai had faces that were difficult to read. It wasn't so much that they were expressionless, only that Cassie and Baron were still not versed in Mahrainian culture, and had only caught on to a few gestures and expressions. Still, they were often clueless.

"We have located them," Dar said. His face was quite solemn according to Cassie and Baron's interpretation, but he bowed his head, murmured a few Mahrainian words before engaging them directly.

"They are safe. That is all that we can tell you now."

Cassie let out a squeal and hugged Baron. They held each other, rocked back and forth, then wiped tears away from each others cheeks. Baron didn't care if Dar and the others saw him cry. He had never felt so relieved in his life. To be so loved and protected, then to have all that yanked away.

"When can we see them?" they asked in unison, and Dar shook his head. He had, after all, spent a considerable amount of time on Haura, and when needed, or when he remembered, would use Hauran gestures.

"I do not know. But they are safe, and that is what is important, is it not?"

Cassie and Baron nodded their heads.

Another person entered the room. Security, obviously, as he was dressed in the same way as Verson and T'ai. *There's way too much security here,* Baron thought, and wondered if they were barricaded in here for safety. What wasn't Dar telling them? Were the Toori here, too? Goosebumps rose on his arms beneath the thin fabric of his shirt, and a flash of the first time he'd seen one of those creatures brought on a brief bout of nausea.

"It seems that the others are not coming. There has been a delay."

"It's not safe!" Cassie yelled out with such command that Dar's eyes widened.

Cassie started to shiver, and her teeth chattered. Then she arched her back, shaking uncontrollably. Baron reached out for her.

"Ohmagod—she's having a seizure!" Baron cried out. "What do I do? She's never done this before."

Dar tapped something into his handheld device, and several attendants came into the room within seconds to whisk Cassie away.

"This is not a good sign," was all Dar said while tapping his fingers together before laying them flat on the stone table.

Baron looked over at him, closed his eyes, called out to his grandmother. *Grams—we need you! Why aren't you here?*

He wiped away a tear, turned away from Dar to stare out at the darkening sky. Two moons appeared in the distance, and just beyond them, a darker shape that he thought might be Mahrain.

What was awaiting them on the planet where they should have been born to a mother and father, where he and Cassie would have been raised together?

Or if Danyal had told them the truth, where he and Cassie wouldn't have been allowed to be born.

Chapter 18

Baron and Dar sat in silence. From time-to-time, one of his security detail would come into the room, murmur something to him, then leave. All Baron could think about was Cassie. He knew she had a delicate system, but seizures? What had set that off? Being in stasis?

Just before they'd boarded the spaceship—or whatever it was—hadn't Dar said something about them feeling better the closer they were to their homeland, the further away they were from Haura? That seemed years ago—and perhaps it was. . .He didn't feel any different, neither stronger nor weaker. Just the same.

And yet he knew that he was changing in the same way he knew there was something going on. Something unanticipated?

"Please to come with me."

Baron turned to the sound of the voice. One of Dar's security detail gestured for him to rise. Dar was no longer in the room. When had he left? Where had he gone?

"Sure. Where are we going?"

"Ooli has sent for you. She will explain."

Baron followed the man down the hall where they took an elevator to another floor. He couldn't tell whether they went up or down, only that they traveled. It was a strange feeling, but not as strange as everything else that had been going on in his life.

After they stepped out of the elevator, there were more hallways. A lattice-work of them. Smooth walls and smooth floors that seemed to be carved out of rock. Baron reached out a hand to trail along the wall. It was warm to the touch as if it was fitted with central heating. But where—or what—was the source? He didn't see any vents. Were they beneath Poora's surface? Close to hot springs, which meant volcanic action? He tried not to let his thoughts tie him up in knots, as given his present state-of-mind, he'd need some sort of double-edged sword to hack through them. If he wasn't careful, he would be turned inside out with the process. Hadn't his Grams said something like that to him all through his life? He supposed it translated to a "think positive" attitude, but now he wondered if it was a Mahrainian saying.

"We are here." The security detail bowed slightly in front of an open room. Ooli was waiting for him. Without even thinking about it, he reached out to hug her. She allowed him to hug her, and they stood there for a few moments. Just as he was settling into the warmth and comfort of her, she extricated herself, gestured to a table and chairs. He plopped down in a metal chair, sighed. It was more comfortable than it looked.

"I know you have lots of questions—especially about Cassie now." Ooli sat down next to him, reached out to grab a slice of dried fruit from a platter. "You really should eat something."

Baron nodded, but didn't take anything from the plate. Ooli picked up another piece of fruit, handed it to him. He put it in his mouth, but didn't feel like chewing it. The presence of food in his mouth after so long without it triggered his hunger, though, and he began to salivate. He chewed, and an incredible flavor rose in his mouth. A mixture of apricot and peach and something else. He chewed, swallowed, reached for another piece, then grabbed a handful.

Ooli smiled. "Take it easy. It's good you're responding to food. It does take awhile after stasis."

After eating a few more pieces of fruit, he drank a glass of water, then another. It tasted even better than that expensive water his Grams always got at Whole Foods.

"When can I see Cassie? Is she going to be okay?" he finally asked.

Ooli laid her hands in her lap, fighting the urge to reach out to Baron. "It is irregular, these seizures, as you call them, but not unheard of. Pree, one of our top doctors, or healers, gave her something. She's being monitored and hasn't had another seizure, which is good, isn't it? I just learned that she is sleeping peacefully. This is a good thing." Ooli stopped for a moment to study Baron's face. He turned away, reached for the pitcher to pour himself another glass of water.

"And go easy on the fluid intake, too. You don't want to blow up like a Poochi bug after feeding."

"Poochi bug? What's that?" Baron thought it sounded like a kid's word for something extremely gross.

"Ah, yes. You don't have those on Haura. You'll be filled in on a variety of information that will be necessary once we leave here. Fortunately, the Poochi bugs are hibernating now. You don't have to worry about them."

Baron took a sip of his water, closed his eyes. He was pretty sure he never wanted to see a Poochi bug in or out of hibernation.

"They want to keep her under observation for awhile," Ooli said, "feed her extra nutrients. It was a long journey. We are beyond what you on Haura call the Alpha Centauri system."

Baron nodded, avoided looking into her eyes, stared instead at the smooth rock walls, the shadows cast by an unseen light source.

"It was a long voyage," she said again.

"Where are we now? Underground? I feel like I'm underground. Is this some sort of military fortress?"

Ooli turned to look through the arched doorway where several security staff stood at attention, their dark blue suits like a second skin.

"We are safe here. But yes, we are below ground level now. As to whether this is a fortress, I'm not sure what you mean. This is what you might call a safe house on Haura. We are not military—is that what you meant?"

"Something like that. I know I'm not a prisoner, but I feel like one. We can't go outside, can we?"

Ooli's eyes clouded. She shook her head. "Not here. Not now. I would like to tell you more, but please believe that we are here for your protection."

Baron nodded, reached for his cup, finished the water. It was quite cold, and soothed him. Ooli filled his glass again, watched him for awhile, noticed how tired he looked, how tired and how sad, his eyes cloudy and unfocused.

Baron yawned, stretched, then settled into the chair.

"I feel so tired," he yawned again.

"So sleep, Baron. Sleep," Ooli murmured to him, the sound of her voice soothing, hypnotic. He called out to Cassie—to his Grams—as he began to drift. Waves of amorphous dark lavender and indigo shapes passed through his inner vision, then expanded in all directions.

Chapter 19

Baron.

There was that voice again.

Baron wasn't sure if he was asleep and dreaming until Danyal appeared. It was similar to when he'd contacted them in stasis; but this time, Danyal appeared with more clarity—like those new HD wide-screen TVs. Blue Ray—or whatever they were called. For a moment, Baron's thoughts drifted toward the last time he'd watched something on TV. What had that show been? *Fringe?* There had been these bald-headed guys called The Watchers, or something. They'd looked similar to Dar and Verson. Maybe SF shows were really leaks from an alien source, evidence of an alien presence. He was wondering if he'd ever get to watch TV or DVDs ever again when Danyal called his name.

Baron. Pay attention. Please to Focus.

Okay. I'm here. Baron thought he sounded irritated, thought, *Sorry.*

No worries as you say on Haura. Danyal paused, gestured to a well-worn path that was illuminated by muted green light. *Walk with me. I need to tell you something something of importance.*

Baron noticed how Danyal hesitated before emphasizing the word, "importance", and hoped that Danyal was finally going to give him a few pieces to fill in the ever-expanding puzzle of their existence.

He wanted to ask Danyal about their parents. To corroborate what his Grams and Dar had said, but he couldn't seem to formulate the words. Baron felt his feet move as he walked beside Danyal down the path. He looked at his hands, wriggled his fingers, peered around, and realized that it was a different room, if you could even call it that, than they'd been in before. It was more like a cave, but one that had been altered for habitation or some other purpose. The walls were smooth, with striations of a crystalline, substance. Baron reached out to feel the surface. Warm, like the rooms on Poora. Was Danyal imprisoned on Poora?

So, little brother. There is so much I have to tell you. Very little time. I am ill, as I told you before, and do not know how much longer I will be able to speak with you.

I'm sorry about that. What's wrong?

Even though there was a part of Baron's mind that didn't want to trust Danyal, he wasn't without compassion for this person who claimed to be his and Cassie's older brother, who had not only contacted him and Cassie while they were in stasis, but had been able to transport them to wherever he was.

It is what you might call a genetic disease. Incurable even for our doctors. Some sort of aberration. An anomaly, perhaps. Yes, that is what you might call it. An anomaly. Which is why it is so important that I speak with you. Cassie did not respond to me. Where is she?

So my supposed brother isn't all-knowing, Baron noted, and hoped that Danyal couldn't hear his thoughts. He wanted to get as much information as he could before pressing the issue.

Apparently, Danyal didn't hear his thoughts or ignored them. He was, after all, supposedly their older brother—and that probably meant he deserved respect.

Danyal and Baron reached the end of a path that opened up into a cavern. The surface area itself wasn't that large, but when Baron tilted his head, the space spiraled upward. He could hardly wait to tell Cassie about it.

Cassie drew this place.

She did? Danyal seemed intrigued, tapped his fingers together.

Cassie had a seizure or something. She's being monitored. That's probably why she didn't respond to you.

Danyal sighed. *That is too bad. I hope that she will be okay—that you will both be okay.*

Baron noticed crystal spires. Stalactites? Stalagmites? He couldn't remember which were which, even though he'd taken geology. There was an area just off to the side where they existed in abundance. And was that water he heard bubbling? A stream? A waterfall?

Please follow me. I have something you need to see, and then I will explain what I can.

Baron followed Danyal across the cavern to an opening in the wall. Danyal paused just outside the curved opening, gestured to Baron to enter first. Baron met Danyal's eyes, studied them intently for a moment, saw sadness there, and something else, something indefinable.

I realize you may not trust me yet. Would you feel more comfortable if I went first?

Baron hesitated for a moment, then stepped toward the dark opening, paused to look back at Danyal, who attempted a smile.

Once you see it, you'll understand. It's a puzzle only you and

Cassie can solve. I have failed to live up to my father's—to our father's—expectations. I have failed you and Cassie both.

Baron reached out to rest his hand on his brother's shoulder, but Danyal moved out of the way.

Please—we must not waste any more time.

Baron stepped over the dark threshold with Danyal just a few paces behind him. He had difficulty adjusting to the absence of light, and trusted that his feet were moving forward, that Danyal would guide him if the need arose. It was cool and damp wherever they were, the only sound, the soft scrape of their slippers along the floor, amplified by some sort of resonant properties within the corridor.

Baron—it is just ahead. Your eyes will adjust in a few moments. There—do you see it? That is our commingled destiny—

Chapter 20

Baron awoke with a start. He'd fallen asleep in the chair yet again, and had a sore neck. He crossed his arms over his chest to reach around to massage his neck and shoulders. Once he'd rubbed the worst of the ache out, he stretched, yawned, and looked around the room.

Then he remembered his dream—if that was what it was.

What was Danyal going to tell me—to show me? Baron wondered, feeling more than a bit irritated by his inability to remember his dreams—especially the ones that were obviously important. He could still feel the darkness of that room, or cave, around him, could still see Danyal's pale sick face in front of him. *I've got to remember!*

"Ah—you're finally awake!" Ooli entered the room, grabbed a stool, pulled it closer to the table.

Baron rubbed his eyes, stretched. "I had the strangest dream. . ." He was just going to utter Danyal's name, then caught himself. Even though he and Cassie agreed Ooli was okay, he still wasn't ready to talk about Danyal.

"Cassie?"

"She's still being monitored. Some slight improvement. The doctors think it's just an adjustment period to the gravitational changes, the heavy magnetic energy on this planet. She's not in danger—so try not to worry. They want to keep her sedated."

"Can I see her?"

Ooli nodded. "I think it would be good for her if you were there when she wakes up. It will help ground her."

"Yes, it will be a good idea."

Baron turned around at the sound of Dar's voice. There was another person there. A doctor? The person was androgynous looking, and Baron wondered if he or she were from yet another planet, what with his or her short stature and slender, almost child-like proportions. Even on Earth, or Haura, there were people whose sex was difficult to determine, but the voice was often a give-away.

"This is Pree, Cassie's healer."

Pree cleared his or her throat, said, "Sorry, Hauranspeak not so good. Sister stable more. Yes." Then Pree left the room, his or her voice, not giving any clues, either.

From outside in the hall, Pree called out. "Follow, yes. See sister."

Ooli offered her hand to help Baron out of the chair. She was a lot stronger than she looked, Baron mused, and Ooli smiled in response, obviously hearing him within her mind.

Baron was sure he blushed. "I need to watch my thoughts more closely, don't I?"

Ooli grinned back. "No worries. You'll get used to it. Don't worry so much. I'm not offended—and most of our people just let the small thoughts and observations drift away. It's the major things you want to watch out for." She looked into his eyes, and Baron sensed that Ooli knew he was trying not to think of something—trying not to think about Danyal. Did she already know about him?

Ooli didn't give him any sort of acknowledgement, but pulled away from their eye-lock and started walking toward the door.

And then it hit him. Pree had referred to Cassie as his sister. They all knew and probably just assumed that he and Cassie knew as well.

With Pree leading, Dar walked just ahead of Baron and Ooli toward the lift that would take them to Cassie. Once again, Baron had no idea if they were traveling up or down—even sideways—through the structure. He was even more certain that they were housed in some sort of compound hewn out of rock as everywhere they went, the walls were made of the same substance. It didn't look like concrete. Perhaps it was some kind of mixture of concrete and stone. And where were all the windows? The only one he'd seen was in that meeting room. There were probably others, but he had no idea where the others were—or even where he was. If Ooli said, "you can go back to your room," he would have no idea how to get there. If he didn't know better, he would believe that he and Cassie were the prisoners, as they were guarded everywhere they went. Dar had their safety in mind—he was sure of that—but he wondered if he'd ever be left totally alone. Perhaps privacy was a foreign concept to these aliens, he mused, then realized that he was an alien, too. How fast life changes. He was sure his Grams had a saying for that, too, but it eluded him.

Pree waved his hand over a panel. There was a small whoosh of air, like an exhalation, when the lift door opened, and Baron wondered if they were in some sort of isolation chamber. Since his Grams had taken such good care of him, and since he'd never been in an accident, he'd never been to a doctor, much less a hospital. He had no idea what to expect, even on Haura, except for what he saw on TV and in movies or books. The last thing he was expecting was to be in a room like this.

Baron expected to see Cassie sleeping in something resembling a bed, or even an incubator of some kind. Instead, he was taken aback by this odd structure. She was encased in layers of what looked like gauze and suspended from the ceiling like a chrysalis on the underside of a leaf. The ceiling itself pulsed with various shades of alternating lights, first purple, then blue, then a golden orange. Even with the light beaming down on her, Cassie looked so pale.

Pree gestured to a bench-like structure, and when Baron sat down, it conformed to him. He remembered this bench from when they'd first met Danyal.

"I'll stay with you—if you like. . ." Ooli said, hesitating before she sat down on another bench facing his.

"That would be nice," was all he could say, staring at Cassie beneath those strange pulsing lights, her pale face contorted with some sort of nightmare—or pain—like when one of her headaches was coming on. There was sweat glistening on her forehead, and Baron resisted the impulse to ask for a cool washcloth to wipe her face. He'd never felt these nurturing urges before Cassie came into his life. She inspired this in him without even trying. He wondered if he'd been born first, or if there was some code wired into him to look out for her. Not that he'd done such a good job of it.

Ooli glanced at Cassie, then at Baron, wishing she could do something to make him feel better. Only Cassie waking would do that, she realized. Cassie waking and being okay—being more than okay.

Baron reached his hand out, brushed it against Ooli's. "Thank you," he murmured. Ooli stared at her hand for the longest time; it tingled where Baron's skin had met hers. She closed her eyes, savored the feeling. When she opened them, Baron was studying her.

There it was again. That electric current passing between them. Baron blushed, turned toward Cassie, fought the urge to reach out to her.

He realized that Ooli had been the first girl he'd hugged. He wanted to hug her again, but felt that it would be weird to do it in front of Cassie. His growing attraction to Ooli was embarrassing enough as it was. Ooli must know he was drawn to her—okay, attracted to her something major. He hadn't felt that urge before—and the only "girls" he'd hugged had been Cassie and the two Grams.

Ooli slid off her stool, sat next to Baron. The bench conformed to accommodate her as she moved even closer, leaned against him.

She'll be okay. Your Grams, too. Try not to worry.

Baron nodded without looking at her, tears collecting along the rim of his eyes. He didn't wipe them away, but focused his energy—his will—on Cassie.

Wake up. Be okay. Wake up. Be Okay. The words a mantra within his mind.

Pree walked into the room, rested his hand on Ooli's shoulder. She turned at the touch, rousing Baron from his feverish focus on Cassie.

"Baron. Pree needs us to leave for awhile. Dar wants to talk with you—with us. We can come back later."

He was slow to respond, but as he made to stand up, Ooli was there once again to help him to his feet.

"You should really sleep, too, Baron. After we meet with Dar. You need your rest if you're going to be there for Cassie—*And everything else coming your way,* she thought, but didn't say aloud. Ooli wondered how much of what she thought transferred to Baron. At this point, his mind was clouded with a variety of emotions, and she wouldn't be surprised if very little made its way into his mind.

"I suppose you're right. Any news about the Grammsies? I still don't sense mine—and I can't stop hoping they're waiting just down the hall for us."

"I know it must be difficult. But they are safe. We just can't tell you where they are—yet. I'm sure Dar has some news."

"That would be cool. I could really use a Blaster about now." He grinned, and it almost reached his eyes.

"I'll see what we can find. Coffee is almost a universal constant, you know. Plus, we had a major stash for the café."

Baron smacked his lips. He needed water, too. Instead of asking for some, he asked her another question.

"Why are my dreams being blocked—and by what? I can't seem to remember them except in snippets, and even though I don't usually remember all of them, the ones I do are in vivid color. It's like there's some sort of interference, like my senses have all been turned off."

Ooli was surprised by his question, as her mind had been infused with his need for water—and coffee. Through the fog of his, or was it her, mind, though, Baron detected a glimmer of a thought transference, which she began to release, then pulled back.

"Dar will explain it. It's not my place. Not to get all cryptic on you, but there are forces at work here that even I don't understand. I'm more like a glorified assistant than anything else. It's that proverbial need-to-know like you have on Haura."

Chapter 21

"First of all, Baron," Dar said while pouring him a cup of water, "we realize that you have many questions. We are not, as you have probably surmised, attorneys in the usual sense of the word, but we were advisors to your and Cassie's parents, Lady Galana and Lord Bahar, and then to your grandmothers. 'Lady' and 'Lord' probably aren't the best translations, though. Suffice it to say, they were descendents of an ancient lineage who carried the secret of the Waters of Nyr—and bore that knowledge's burden."

"We didn't know we were brother and sister. It all adds up, though. What else is there that we don't know? And now the burden falls on us? Sounds like a fairy tale to me." He sighed, wondering what Cassie would say to this. Images of her lying in the hospital—or whatever it was called here on Poora—wove in-and-out of his mind. He imagined that if she were here, she'd wind her thick honey-blond hair into a knot, tug at, then release it. If they were back on Haura, she'd probably exclaim that she needed to hurl.

"We would expect you to be skeptical—at first—but please hear us out." Dar paused, seemed to listen to the footsteps coming toward them from down the hall. Whoever it was didn't even pause, but continued on past their room.

"You deserve to know more about your heritage, about the forces of play—" and he turned toward Ooli, as if to acknowledge her earlier words to him. "We cannot possibly tell you everything now, but what we can tell you is this—" Dar looked Baron directly in the eyes, which was something he had rarely done with Baron, then closed them, to collect his thoughts. Even after nearly twenty years on Haura, it was still difficult for him to think, and to find just the right words, in English. He lifted his hands from his lap, extended them, palms up, to Baron.

"You and Cassie are the ones who will unlock the location of the Waters of Nyr. Your combined gifts, which you will learn to further develop, will make it so. That is why it was decided you needed to be born and raised on Haura—and why you had to leave it. That is why your grandmothers, your surrogate mothers, are in what you'd call protective custody, as their proximity to you would endanger them as well. We are still sorry that the team who collected them had to act swiftly—in haste—so that it caused you worry. Besides the Toori—

who are quite skilled in ah—what is that word? Where is T'ai when I need him?"

Dar paused, extended his hands out again, as if the word would appear inside them.

Ooli sent him the word, *torture*, but Dar chose not to say it aloud. He didn't want to add to Baron's obvious distress, and the images that rose in his mind of what the Toori were capable, made even him shudder. He willed himself to dispel a series of horrendous images.

"I'm sorry, Dar, but this is really starting to sound like one of those bad plots for a made-for-TV series." If Cassie were here, he thought, she'd probably say, "See! I told you we were in the witness protection program!"

More like the Alien Protection Program, he mused ironically. Baron needed to walk. He wasn't used to being cooped up like this. They weren't able to go outside because it was barely above freezing and unsafe for reasons other than the weather. He missed going to the Star Gazer café, his bedroom looking out onto the garden where his peppercorn tree had been a magical place. He'd spent some time mentally re-drawing the alien landscapes from his and Cassie's dreams, but the images wouldn't hold still, and had begun to fade from the corners of his mind. He wondered how long they'd been gone from Haura, too. How long they'd been here at this compound, imprisoned ostensibly for their own safety—but until when?

Baron stood up. All he could think about was running out of this room, running out of this structure—but to where? He was light years away from the place—the planet—he had always known as home.

Dar gestured downward with a hand, and Baron sat back down. He immediately detected the scent of freshly brewed espresso and perked up as an attendant walked through the door with a decanter and several cups. He stopped by Baron first, set the stoneware cup in front of him, and poured the thick delicious brew. Baron studied him, and thought he looked familiar. The attendant from the starslip. The one who had placed he and Cassie in stasis. The attendant kept his eyes forward, on the task, then set a cup in front of Ooli and poured. When he was through with pouring their coffee, he set the tray to their right and bowed out of the room.

Should he ask Dar? Hadn't Cassie felt weird around that guy? Or maybe he just couldn't place all these new faces, as they bounced in-and-out-of-focus like a broken kaleidoscope.

"The reason you both were placed in separate surrogates was to protect you and Cassie. You still share consciousness, I believe you would call it, but you are not twins. Before your parents died, their seed was extracted and stored in the hopes that a child or children would some day be born to or for them. Together, you both form a key. Separate, you would be unable to use that key. There are back-up measures in place, but we still need you both—and to get you to safety on Ranat. They are better equipped to help you there."

"But what about that story Grams used to tell me, that our grandmothers told us? "I mean, if the Waters of Nyr are medicine—or something good—why don't we just share them?"

Dar's eyes darkened, his brows furrowed. "What is medicine for one person, is death for another. And there are those who would threaten your very lives to gain access to it."

Dar placed his palms down on the table, and a ripple of what Baron thought appeared to be pain flowed across his face.

"I suppose it is time I told you of your uncle Hamar, your father's younger brother. He is the head of Trilune, which holds multiple interests. The closest you have on Haura would be a multinational conglomerate—only in our sense, it is trans-galactic. Among other divisions, they have major mining projects, and your uncle, your father's brother, Hamar, is what you would call a corporate raider—or embezzler. He seized control from your father, and has been engaging in unethical mining practices, as well as other heinous acts. He does not care if he trammels upon forbidden—or hazardous—worlds to get what he wants." Dar walked over to the window, paused. "Some believe that he was behind your parents' death—and that of his own wife, mother to his son."

Baron wished that the window had been open like it had been yesterday. He needed to see something other than blank walls. Didn't anyone believe in adornment or anything? No art on the walls. No decorations. Just blank stone walls. At least the desert had a few scattered plants and intriguing rock formations.

Baron's days were all jumbled up, probably because he hadn't slept since they'd been out of stasis except for that short nap while he and Ooli sat with Cassie.

How long had he been asleep, though? Time definitely moved differently here on Poora. How many hours in a day on this moon? How much daylight? Darkness? And why, after all that time in stasis, was he still so tired. He yawned, stretched, yawned again, certain that the days were shorter.

"Things aren't that different on other worlds, are they?" Baron asked. He must have sounded beyond sad, almost despairing, as Ooli placed her hand on top of his and left it there. Baron felt his entire body suffuse with warmth. He turned to her, smiled, mouthed "thank you".

"He conducted clandestine operations on Sihar Meh Toh, an off-limits planet, all in search of the Waters of Nyr."

"So it's not medicine?"

"No, it is not. But it is valuable—more valuable than the hematite on Haura and Mooru, or Mars, as you call it, more valuable than the Mora Blossom honey and elixirs from the steppes of Boort, even more valuable than the crystals and gems found within the Poochi hives that extend well beneath Boort.

"I don't even know what any of those things are—except Hematite sounds familiar. It's a smooth black stone or something, right. So what is it then—and why all the mystery?"

Baron noticed that he'd been clenching and unclenching his hands, a habit he'd never had before. At first, he thought it was just a nervous tic he'd developed from stasis, but now he realized it was a sign of anger and frustration. Neither emotion was familiar to him, and Baron realized that he—that they—had lead a very pampered existence until recently. There were still vestiges of that evident here on Poora. Not only was Baron's world being turned upside down, but it was being stretched like a canvas to the four corners of the galaxy. Any moment now, he feared that it would begin to tear.

"It is you, Baron. And Cassie. You are the Waters of Nyr."

"What the—" Baron was stunned. "How can we be the Waters of Nyr?"

"Because of your birthright, your parentage. It is also because you and Cassie are among a small group of children born to Mahrain after nearly fifty of your Hauran years. . ."

It was then Baron knew he had to tell Dar about Danyal. There was no way his supposed brother was that old.

Chapter 22

"There's something I need to tell you, Dar," Baron began.

He'd been rehearsing how to tell Dar about Danyal since he'd awakened. Was it morning on Poora? Evening? The middle of the night? Back home, he'd had clocks and could peer through the curtains or shutters to get an idea of the time of day. Here, there were no such luxuries—and if there were, he didn't have access to them. What with the artificial light that illuminated the compound, it could be day or night. It wasn't like he had to get up to go to school anymore, but not being on a regular schedule was disconcerting.

Fortunately, the guard had waited outside while he slept—or at least that's what Baron believed. It was difficult for him to sleep when he knew someone was watching him, but he supposed that the guard could have waited until he was asleep to come back into the small room that he had only shared with Cassie for a few hours before she'd had her seizure. The bed was comfortable, though, and a part of him wanted to crawl back into it to sleep some more.

Why did he even need a guard? Wasn't the compound safe? Were there areas that were actually off-limits to him and Cassie? Not that Cassie would go exploring—especially now—but he was curious about this place. Why wasn't Dar—or even Ooli—taking him on the grand tour? He knew they probably wouldn't be here long, that it was just a stopping place within a larger journey.

Or maybe this was all there was to the compound: a latticework of hallways leading to other hallways with an occasional small suite of rooms for sleeping or meeting. He doubted it. He sensed—no, he knew—that this place had to be huge. It wasn't all docking bays and spaceship hangars. It wasn't all corridors leading to more corridors leading to an occasional room. There was much more to this place, and Baron was curious about what else was housed here.

Or who else.

He ran wet hands through his hair, realized that it was much longer than he remembered. Much, much longer. . .almost down to his waist. Doing a few mental calculations, he realized that he and Cassie must have been in stasis for at least three months, if not longer.

But how long had they been on Poora? Two days? Three? A week? Or was this still the same day they arrived? He wondered how many hours in a day, weeks in a month, months in a year on this moon. It was probably all different than Haura. It had to be.

Since Baron had never had to shave, which hadn't bothered him in the least, the length of his hair was a definite sign of time passing. He'd lost weight, too, which was another sign, and probably a good thing, as Grams' cooking had always been way too good to say, "no" to seconds—or even thirds. Then there had been all those trips to The Star Gazer for coffee and sweets.

He sighed. Grams' cooking. His mouth watered with the memory of her rich stews and home-made breads with sweet butter and cherry jam. He missed hugging her the most, the day-to-day-ness of their lives. He'd been happy. Now he didn't know what he was.

And then he felt her presence, heard her within his mind.

I miss you, too, sweetie.

Grams! Where are you? How are you? Cassie and I have been worried sick. How's her Grams?

We're safe. Please don't worry. How is Cassie? Is she better? Iliana sends her love and hugs to both of you.

You know about that? Oh, yeah, Dar is in contact with you.

Baron was relieved to finally hear from her. It was like an anchor to their past life.

You two weren't prepared for this. We are so sorry. We thought there was more time. Please forgive us.

Don't worry about it, Grams. We're okay. And Ooli from the Stargazer Café is here. And oh—Ms. Brunhof, that art teacher Cassie liked—she's a shape-shifting monster.

Yes, I know, but please trust Dar. I know you two must wonder whom to trust right now—even whether you should trust us—but Dar will do his best to see you safely home to us.

His Grams didn't respond to his *And to fulfill our destiny?*

and Baron hoped he didn't sound sarcastic. He wasn't angry at her—how could he be? She loved him and cared for him—protected him from whatever all these forces were. Then, he remembered his nagging question.

Grams? We know we're brother and sister now, and wish you'd told us sooner anyway. We just knew we were connected, but do we also have an older brother named Danyal?

There was a long pause before she responded.

Where did you hear that name?

He contacted us while we were in stasis—and then I had one of those lucid dreams where he wanted to show me something but I didn't remember what it was when I woke up.

There was another long pause before his Grams responded.

Danyal is not your older brother. He was your Uncle Hamar's son. Did he say he was your brother? Are you sure?

Yes. I'm positive.

After another long pause, his Grams continued. *We thought he was dead. Promise me you'll speak to Dar about this—immediately. And if Danyal tries to contact you again, do your best not to tell him what I told you.*

And he told us he was imprisoned or in exile or something. That our parents weren't dead but held captive with him.

Oh sweetie. How I wish that were true. They have truly passed on, but you are their seed. You are definitely from their seed, and so is Cassie. Iliana and I were honored to carry, give birth to, and raise you. Hold that in your heart. Don't forget our love for you both is deeper than the Mora Sea.

Chapter 23

Dar was in the meeting room, seated with eyes closed, hands resting in his lap, when Baron was first ushered through the door. Baron noticed that it was warmer in here today, and was grateful for his light-weight pajama outfit. Beads of perspiration rose along his back and chest, then dissipated. He wondered if there was something special about the lapis blue cloth, and lifted it away from his chest to check for nonexistent damp spots. He pressed a wrist against his forehead. He wasn't feverish, but he definitely felt flushed.

Baron was going to sit down on the opposite end of the table so as not to disturb Dar's meditation when Dar opened his eyes, nodded toward the coffee.

"I could really use some of this." Baron reached for the pot, poured himself a cup. Even the scent began to unclog his brain. He took a sip, then another, smacked his tongue appreciatively.

"Your surrogate, excuse me, your grandmother, Selene, has told me you have been in contact, that there is a matter of some urgency."

Baron could feel heat rise to his face again. Was he nervous, even embarrassed about not saying anything earlier? After all, this stuff was serious, and besides, Dar had done so much for them. . .

"I'm sorry we didn't mention Danyal earlier, but Cassie and I—we just didn't know if we should. He asked us not to." He paused to take another sip of the hot coffee, held it in his mouth before swallowing. "He was quite adamant about it, said our safety was at stake."

"As Selene said, we believe Danyal to be dead. In fact, we are certain of it. He died before you and Cassie were even born. It was devastating to his mother, but his father. . ." Dar's voice trailed off as he resisted the impulse to be ensnared in an old memory that clung to him like a Mora spider to a thick petal.

"He was always ill as a boy, and became more ill as a young man. . ." Dar paused to reflect on his next words. He wished that Baron—and Cassie, too—had more advanced skills with mindspeak. This would develop with time, he knew, but they didn't have the luxury to wait for that eventuality. How much should he tell him now? That was the issue. So much had transpired in so little time on Poora, and very little had gone according to plan.

Dar stood, walked to the window, pressed open the shield

covering, pointed to a slight rise in the distance. It was covered with great slabs of stone and sparse vegetation that clung to the ground, sapping whatever moisture was there. Baron stood up and walked to the window.

"Do you see those rocks, Baron? Just beyond that seemingly innocuous configuration is a network of tunnels much like where we are now. Beneath them is an old section of this base. We had closed it off due to some structural issues. We thought that it was totally abandoned, that none of our people were still there, but after noticing some activity, we discovered a Toori presence."

Dar examined Baron's face for signs of comprehension. "It's possible, no, it's definite that your uncle Hamar has something to do with this."

"So—are we about to be attacked?"

"This we do not know," Dar replied, continuing to scan the distance for visual evidence. He turned to face Baron. "There are many ways to wage an attack—and not just a physical one. It is possible that Hamar is having one of the Toori assume the form of his son. Something familiar, someone familiar, to lure you and Cassie to them. I doubt that Hamar is absolutely aware of what you both know. He may be testing you."

Dar paused, leaned forward to rest his hands on Baron's shoulders, their weight enough to cause Baron to lean forward, lose his balance, then right himself.

"It would be much easier for the Toori to approach you with mindthought, to just send an image rather than assume Mahrainian form with a synthsuit. I am sorry, Baron, but your cousin, Danyal, is no longer alive. This we know for certain. It is very important, Baron, that you remember what you told this Danyal. What did he say to you? How much does he know about you and Cassie? What did he show you? Did you share any information about this base? Allow your mind to open to me—please—so that I can know what you know."

"I'll try," Baron said.

"You don't need to try to do anything. Just allow it to happen and don't resist."

Baron set his coffee cup down. "What do I do?"

"Sit down. Relax. Now close your eyes. Good. Now take a breath, let it out slowly. Take another, let it out slowly, then try to push as much of your air out. That's good. One more. Focus on releasing all that stale air. Good. Now breathe normally."

Dar sat down in front of Baron, noticed that he seemed much

more relaxed. "Lean back. You don't need to sit up so straight. Just relax. Keep breathing."

Baron felt the jolt as Dar penetrated his mind. Even though he wanted to be helpful, he still struggled at the sensation. It felt like an assault, as it was nothing like this with his Grams. She was gentle, flowed in-and-out of his mind like the scent of star blooming jasmine on a summer evening, or the scattering of fall leaves on the ground. But Dar was like a tropical storm wrenching at palm fronds and whipping them aloft. Baron tried not to struggle, to allow Dar to find what he needed, but everything in his being fought against it.

And then, just as he thought he couldn't resist any longer, release. . .His thoughts and memories, sensations and emotions, began to sort themselves into categories, forming networks of information, then a steady stream of data. Baron sighed, relaxed, as Dar continued to look for the information he needed.

It's like dreaming, Baron thought. No longer resisting the process, he watched with mounting curiosity. It was like watching a movie which occasionally froze, was rewound, only to be fast-forwarded, then allowed to be played without interruption.

Time moved differently in this realm of the mind as well, and it seemed like nearly an hour had passed before Dar finally accessed the dream from the other day, the dream where Danyal was trying to show him something, when Danyal had claimed to have something important to tell him.

Just as abruptly, Baron sensed, then saw, Cassie in the dream with him. He hadn't remembered that, and now he knew why. . .

Walking through the archway, his eyes adjusting to the darkness just enough to see Cassie with Danyal. He peered closer, and now he knew why he didn't want to remember the dream. . .

Danyal was gone, and in his place, standing with its pasty tentacle of an arm around Cassie, a Toori!

Baron struggled forward, reaching out to grab the Toori in his mind and felt a hand gently pressing him back into the chair.

Keep looking around, Baron. What else do you see? We need to help Cassie, to find out where they are, what they're planning. Do you see anything else there? Anyone else? Landmarks? Can you tell if they are here in this compound? Somewhere else close by?

Baron extended his awareness, sank deeper into the memories of his dreamwalk. The cave appeared in his mind. Damp and dark with iridescent fungi on the walls that emitted a pale light. He scanned the area behind where the Toori was talking to Cassie. She was standing up. She was okay, but she couldn't move. Something was preventing her from moving. And in the distance, a passageway. Someone leaning against the passage opening, but they were blurry. More Toori in uniform. He could make out an insignia: three circles over a curved line. There was someone else, someone not Toori, or not appearing to be a Toori. He was wearing those loose pajamas with a dark robe covering them, and holding a device that looked just like the one Verson carried around. It pulsated with a green light, dimmed as it appeared to alter frequencies.

Baron peered closer and then with a flash, the man disappeared. It was just like when the Toori was following him and Cassie, when Verson had pushed them both out of the way.

Baron opened his eyes into Dar's. "Is that everything?" he asked, his body-mind feeling drained despite the prickle of rising anger. He wondered if Dar could see things that he wasn't even aware of. Clearly he could.

Dar tapped his fingers together.

"It is enough. They have one of our devices. That's how they were able to come on to the base. That cave is close by nevertheless, and I recognize the man in the robe."

He switched to mindspeak. *It is your Uncle Hamar—which means that he is here on Poora as well.*

Chapter 24

Cassie struggled to wake up. She had to climb out of this horrendous dream. Could it be true? Had Danyal lied to them? In here, he was a shape-shifting monster like Ms. Brunhof. Not their brother, not their brother, not their brother. Baron was her brother, not this monster!

In the way that she knew things, the family gift her Gramma Iliana referred to all the time, she knew that this dream was real. "Dreams don't lie," her Gramma had said. "But sometimes, they reveal truth in another way so that you will recognize it."

Cassie remembered feeling cold, shaking violently. Someone—it was Baron—had said she was having a seizure. She'd never had a seizure before. What was wrong with her? A part of her awareness remained focused on how she was in a hospital or something like that, cared for by gentle hands. She remembered feeling warm. Wonderfully warm. The shaking had stopped, and she had drifted asleep, feeling peaceful and safe. Yes, peaceful and safe.

And then Danyal was there. Just like he'd been in stasis, only more clear, as the room wasn't suffused with that odd mist. He'd taken her hand, asked her to walk with him, but his hand had felt all wrong, not like a hand at all. Not human. She had brushed this observation away, realizing it was just a dream, and he was her older brother. She wanted to get to know him, to learn about their parents, to learn about him.

They continued to walk together. The only sound a distant humming. She couldn't smell a thing, which was odd, as her dreams usually flourished with scents both familiar and strange.

Where's Baron? She'd asked Danyal, but he didn't respond, just smiled and walked faster. How could Danyal be walking so fast? Before, he'd been lethargic, in obvious pain, and contacting them had been a major effort for him, visibly draining his energy. Was he feeling better? Had someone found a cure at long last for whatever disease he had?

Or had it all been an act to gain sympathy?

I have something to show you, Cassie. Something important. You'll see when we get there. You'll see. Danyal's voice was soothing, friendly. There was nothing to worry about. She was with her older brother.

And then he pushed her roughly through an archway. She stumbled, started falling. The effort to break the fall jolted her abruptly awake. Her heart was pounding, her breath was labored, and she began to shudder violently.

Not another seizure!

Her eyes readjusted to the room, and she saw Pree, reached out for him, but her hands were confined. Why was she confined? Pree rushed to her side, looked into her eyes, said something in mindspeak she didn't understand. He made a cooing sound, stroked her hair, then began to administer another sedative. Didn't he realize she was in danger, that she had to stay awake? Why was he keeping her sedated when she had to wake up?

Her heart rate began to slow down to a healthy pace, her breathing, too, as the sedative took affect, infusing her with warmth, her body no longer shaking.

And then she was in that dark space again. The cave walls emanating a pale green light. Danyal was there. Danyal and yet not Danyal. His appearance shifted along the edges, became someone else—some *thing* else!

Toori! She screamed in her mind. *She was being held by the Toori!*

The thing that had been Danyal grinned, and it was not a pleasant sight.

Chapter 25

Time no longer stood still for Baron as the station rose to action. Three teams of blue-suited security, one led by Verson, another by T'ai, and the third by a man Baron hadn't seen before, gathered in the meeting room and outside along the corridor. One of the units was sent to guard Cassie and Pree, another was sent to check the various access and exit points. The third was awaiting Dar's instructions, which were to prepare to leave for Ranat as soon as possible.

Somehow the Toori had gained access to their compound and Hamar was on Poora.

While Dar had been sifting through Baron's mind for memories and other information, he had locked inner eyes with a Toori, who was simultaneously attempting to access Baron's mind during their session.

The supposedly abandoned structure was not merely showing signs of a Toori presence, it was definitely active. This also meant that he was right. One of the crew members aboard the ship that brought them here to Poora had also been Toori. They couldn't have accessed Baron and Cassie's mind during stasis otherwise.

But who?

When Dar had shared this information with Baron, he had tapped his fingers together, eyes closed, creating, rearranging, and rechecking lists in his mind. *Who on board their ship? Who on board their ship?* He probed, but the answer wasn't forthcoming. Whoever it had been was quite skilled with shape shifting, and could hold an alien form for long periods of time without showing signs of collapse. It wasn't a matter of just wearing a synthsuit. This one shifted, and could hold a Mahrainian form even within deep space. He would have known if any of his crew were wearing a synthsuit.

Baron wished that he could help, that he knew who the impersonator was. He also wished he'd been able to see his uncle more clearly, but the man's face had been in shadow. Dar, however, had recognized him immediately.

At the time they'd boarded, they'd all been in such a rush, frightened, freaked-out, but once they'd boarded, these feelings had dissipated for the most part. He couldn't recall feeling anything—or anyone—out of place as his whole world was already going wonky. Perhaps Cassie could—or would—remember. Baron remembered that

Cassie had glanced strangely at one of the stasis attendants, but at that time, everything was non-stop strange for the two of them.

It couldn't be Ooli. It just couldn't.

Pree? No, Pree vibrated at another frequency altogether. He was a healer. There was no way it was Pree.

One of the guards? No way! Baron realized that that would be impossible, especially with their rigorous training and schedule. From what he now knew of the Toori, most of them had to wear fake skin, that synthsuit, in order to sustain another form. They could shapeshift, but not for long periods of time.

Now he knew why Ms. Brunhof looked all mangled up once in awhile, more so toward the end of the semester. She hadn't been able to hold it together—especially when she had one of those headaches. He wondered if there was anyone here on Poora with excruciating headaches. That might be a sign. The environment, despite it being winter, was similar to earth's, to Haura's.

Ooli rushed into the room, interrupting Baron's attempts to solve this puzzle. She grabbed his shoulder more roughly than she intended.

"Ouch!" Baron yelped, automatically reaching to push her away.

"Sorry. But you need to come with me. Dar sent me to get you. We're going to Ranat **now**. It's not safe here any longer."

"That's an understatement. Okay," Baron said, rubbing his shoulder and arm where her vice-of- a-hand had clamped onto him. He noticed her face was flushed, and that she was almost out-of-breath. How far had she run? Or was she just stressed, adrenalin pumping through her body? She did have adrenalin, didn't she? He wondered for a fleeting moment about how his body—and Cassie's—were different than humans. No one had shared that bit of information with them yet, either.

With Ooli setting the pace, Baron followed as fast as he could, just a few paces behind her, through an unfamiliar corridor. Since Baron had only seen a minute portion of the station since they'd arrived on Poora, there was probably much more to this compound than he would see this time—or ever. Ooli definitely knew her way around, though, and he wondered if she'd lived here before opening the Star Gazer café on Haura.

Baron noticed that this corridor was much more narrow and constricted than the others, and was made of a different material—what, he didn't know, as it was unlike anything he'd seen before. The porous rock had been leveled and polished like the other walls, but this one was interspersed with a collage of smooth black stones that glistened in the ambient light. He touched them as he hurried along, and felt them warm to his touch. Hematite, he remembered. These stones were hematite. But why were they only in this corridor?

He and Ooli were definitely descending. The lighting dimmed, and Baron's ears began to itch and throb the further they descended. They were right outside what looked like a dead end when Ooli pressed her hands against the wall and it slid inside itself.

Baron was amazed. He didn't see any sign to show that there was a door or any other type of entrance here.

And then his ears started ringing. No, they weren't ringing. Something else was happening. Alternating cold and hot trickles, then streams, of energy flowed up the sides of his head, suffusing the crown of his head with a strange sensation. It felt like blood—or some other substance—was flowing unchecked just beneath his skin. He rubbed at his ears, his neck, shook his head a few times in an attempt to clear the high-pitched whine that had begun to oscillate within his ears.

"What is that sound?" he cried out to Ooli, who turned to him, her face not appearing to register the question.

"My ears, they feel like they're going to explode," he said.

"That's the ship warming up. You can feel that?" She smiled, and Baron thought she also seemed relieved.

"Perhaps you'll be a starslip pilot after all."

Baron thought that her response was odd. No one had ever said anything about him being a pilot—and what did his sensitivity have to do with flying a starship?

And then there it was. . .The starslip. Baron had never seen anything so bizarre and so wondrous in his entire life. It was about twenty feet long and shaped more like a seed cone than a ship. It pulsed with an eerie light, the outer hull porous, nearly transparent, like the molted skin of a lizard or snake.

But it was puny compared to the other ship they'd arrived on. Much too small to accommodate everyone. Much too small.

"Yes," Ooli said, responding to Baron's thoughts. "It's just you and me on this one. The others will follow."

"But Cassie—what about Cassie?"

Ooli didn't know what, or how much, to tell him. How could she look him in the eyes and lie? Cassie would be left behind with Pree and a protective duty, until they could sever the Toori's connection on her mindbody. She knew he wouldn't come with her if she told the truth, but if Baron were also captured by the Toori. . .That could not happen!

"Dar said we have to leave now. Pree will prepare Cassie for transport on another ship. Come on. We have to go now. You will see her on Ranat."

Ooli gave Baron a gentle nudge toward the starslip. He took a step toward it, then another, his head humming with the energetic pulse emanating from the craft. Even his body felt strange, as if it were coming apart at the seams, becoming something else, something other than his body. He was being drawn toward the ship. . .he had to get to the ship. . .to be inside the ship. It took all his willpower to stop his body moving toward it.

Baron reached out his hands to stop Ooli, to get her to wait. "Hey—who's flying this thing? I remember you said you weren't a pilot."

Ooli locked eyes with him, reached into his mind to calm him, to trigger his repressed knowledge, if possible.

"You are—but it basically flies itself. I'll be your co-pilot."

Chapter 26

While en route to Ranat, Baron and Ooli were wide awake. Ooli studied Baron as he gazed through the viewport at the landscape of space, mesmerized.

"Interested in a bit of astronomy?" she asked.

"Sure—so long as you keep it simple."

Ooli took a sip of water, clutched the container between her thighs as she directed his gaze to the left. "You see that cluster of stars? That's the Poochi Bug Nebula."

"I don't even know what the bugs look like, so what's what?"

"See how that cluster of stars forms a body, tapered at the end. Those lines of stars, there are two strands on opposite ends of the body. Those are its front digging claws. They're burrowers. Part of our import-export system. Nasty bugs, but without them, a large chunk of Mahrain's TGP, or trans-galactic profit, would be lost."

"Do I dare ask why they make big money? What's that planet there—or is it a moon?" Baron pointed to a dark gray sphere to the right, swirling with what looked like a bank of fog.

"That's Soola. Another one of Mahrain's moons. Just the Sisterhood live there now.

"The Sisterhood? Like nuns or something?"

"Or something," Ooli murmured. "I'm not sure where they come from originally. Maybe all over. They're advisors of some kind. They supposedly see the future, so politics as usual. Not too many people visit there unless they have to, as they have major tidal seasons interspersed with regular tidal seasons. Lots of storms with the usual lightning, thunder, and rain. No one can be outside during those and survive."

"How many moons does Mahrain have? Cassie would always get fixated on these landscapes with three moons. Memories of Mahrain or something?"

"Actually, Mahrain has more than three moons, but there are three major ones. Poora, where we just left, Soola, and then there's Bejar, the smallest of those three."

"What's on Bejar?"

Ooli shrugged. "Not sure. Never been there. I used to spend quite a bit of time with Dar on Soola. I was supposed to go recently, but then the trip was postponed. Even though I was disappointed, it's a pretty stark life there. The Sisterhood are practically prisoners there during the storm season. Come to think of it, there is storm season and storm season, tsunamis, I think you call them, occur only once in a long while, but the waves are more than slightly daunting most of the time.

Dar goes there pretty regularly, though, as there are some sort of retreat spaces there or something. He always comes back from there looking more centered."

Maybe he has a girlfriend there, Baron thought, but did not say. He grinned at the thought of Dar dating, wondered what sort of woman Dar would go for. "I think centered is his middle name. The guy rarely seems anxious—even with all the stuff going on."

"It's his training or his nature. Not sure which. Probably both. As long as I've known him, he's always been like that."

"So what else can you tell me—whoa! What was that?" Baron leaned as far forward as he could to see the streak of light pass by the starslip. It was followed by two more.

"We call them *pua*. It means tadpoles in Mahrainian. I think you call them shooting stars."

"Why do you call them tadpoles? They don't look like little frogs to me."

"We have a creature that moves like that when it's just past its larval stage. Just like on Haura, there's a metaphor or a story for everything."

"Is that Bejar?" Baron pointed to an ominous dark planet. It reminded him of the Death Star in *Star Wars,* and he wondered if encountering something like that was at all farfetched.

Ooli squinted her eyes to make out the dark orb against a darker section of space. "No, that's another one of the moons, or at least it's occasionally designated as such. There's a mining colony there. Psion IV. Pretty much under Trilune and your uncle Hamar's command. Lots of bars and brothels. Undesirable types, depending upon your view. Still, we get many of our resources there. Hamar has pretty much dug it up looking for the Waters of Nyr."

There was a heavy silence in the starslip's chamber as the words resonated. The Waters of Nyr, Baron thought. None of this would be happening if it weren't for the waters of Nyr.

"Well, he can keep digging, but they're not there," Baron said without thinking. "How'd I know that?" He shrugged, wondering what other bits of information Dar had unleashed when he went digging in his brain. Either that, or he was starting to remember.

"You don't have to talk about it, but if you ever need someone to just listen. . ." Ooli's voice grew softer, and she almost regretted saying anything. She knew the price that had been paid, the price that was even now being paid, to release the waters of Nyr. And here beside her was one third of the key.

Baron turned to her, sighed. "You know, I still don't know what they are. Neither does Cassie. We aren't lying. We don't have a clue. What if the Toori really capture us? What if Uncle Hamar or someone else does? What will they do to us when they realize we don't know a frigging thing?"

Baron growled in frustration, and the sound was so comical that both Ooli and he laughed at once. "What's that Hauran saying? Ours is similar: We'll cross that bridge when we get to it."

"Yeah, but what about thinking ahead? Planning ahead? There's got to be someone who knows."

"There is, Baron. There is. And when the time is right, they'll help you. For now, we just need to make it safely to Ranat."

The two sat in silence while they allowed their attention to just drift through the starscape. Ooli, however, was more focused on scanning the skies for signs that they may be followed. Thus far, they were safely alone.

Baron interrupted the silence first. "What's that constellation?" He pointed to a pattern of stars that outlined an immense humpbacked creature.

"See—you're getting the hang of it. We have passed over or through at least a dozen constellations, but you recognize the one that points toward home. See those series of humps? It's a sea snake undulating through sky waves. You may see one at Ranat."

"What?!" Baron turned around, his narrow eyes rounding.

Ooli giggled. "I couldn't resist that one. There aren't any left at Ranat, not for a long time, but you'll see what we've done with their former habitats."

The starslip angled to prepare its descent. "We're almost there. In a few minutes, the starslip will begin morphing for landing. I just don't want you freaking out on me."

Baron nodded. "So does everything and everyone morph around here? This is getting more familiar, but still strange." He grinned, wondering if Ooli was ever going to morph into something else.

"I heard that—and no, who you see before you is my regular form. Okay. The temp will start rising in here in a few, as we'll be landing underwater. Most of Ranat is submerged, built into the caves. While we aren't going into stasis, there will be some life-support measures coming."

As if on cue, the seats titled back and the air was suffused with warmer air. The temperature began to rise steadily until it leveled off about fifteen degrees warmer.

"Comfy?" She brushed his shoulder with her hand, leaving a trail of goose bumps in its wake. Baron shivered, and wished she'd touch him again, but she didn't. Instead, she pressed back in her own seat.

"Now what?" He covered his mouth with a yawn, stretched, then turned toward her.

"Okay, now the ship will engage its protective stasis. Don't fight it, just allow yourself to surrender to the ship. It wants to protect us from the impact of a water breach as well as the pressure and the frigid water temps."

Before Baron could formulate his next question, a thick blue fluid began to ooze over him from all directions. He yelped, then remembered what Ooli said. "I know, I know. Don't fight it."

"Right. First, it's a fluid, then it becomes tougher and more resilient as a membrane. It aids in maintaining your body heat, as a shock-absorber, and in the event that something should go wrong, it will provide oxygen and other nutrients to your body."

"It does all that?" He shook his head, watching as the fluid flowed over his finger tips, the back of his hands, and moved up his arms.

"Just remember to keep breathing regularly. The last phase is when it covers your head—and yes, your face. You'll still be able to breathe on your own, so don't freak out. It won't suffocate you."

"I'll try not to freak out, Ooli. But this is major weird."

"One of these days, you'll learn more about the starslip, and just in case you're wondering, it's the same material used during long stasis periods."

"So this slime and I are old friends, then?" He smiled brighter than he felt.

"Not this particular slime, but yes, similar. Let's just hope it doesn't know you're insulting it."

"It's alive? Like some sort of parasite?" Baron yelled out, and Ooli sent him some calming energy.

"Actually, you're more of a parasite than it is."

Baron was amused by the irony of the host-parasite relationship, and wanted to say as much, but discovered that he couldn't, as the blue goo had crept up to his throat and was working its way around his chin, up toward his mouth. He clamped his lips shut, breathed erratically through his nose, focused on regulating that, too.

"Oh, I forgot to tell you. Keep your mouth closed," Ooli said, turning toward him, the blue membrane just now reaching her chest. “Looks like you used some common sense. She winked at him, and he winked back. By then, the membrane had completed the first phase of its mission and covered their eyelids with a protective film.

Chapter 27

Dar felt, rather than saw, the starslip depart. Even though Ooli could have piloted the craft, he was relieved that he'd been right. The starslip had sensed Baron, had recognized him even before they'd entered the hangar.

Now that Baron and Ooli were on their way to Ranat, which would take mere moments when compared to their trans-galactic journey from Haura to Poora, he could attend to the next evacuation phase.

Releasing the Toori's hold on Cassie.

What had previously seemed like a seizure even Pree believed was the result of post-stasis acclimation, he now knew was a Toori tactic. He'd never known the Toori to have this ability, and wondered who this Danyal impersonator was and how it was able to get aboard their ship on Haura. Could another clan be assisting Hamar? But which one? The Sisters of the Blood Moon would not assist Hamar. Of that he was sure. If anything, his contacts there would send Hamar to some distant world to search for naught but another vein of semi-precious ores. For now, Hamar's empire building would be limited to tangible commodities. If Hamar had even an inkling that the Sisterhood also held the key, they wouldn't be safe.

Or perhaps he was under-estimating the power of the Sisters of the Blood Moon. Hadn't their ancestors been the first to realize The Water of Nyr's existence? Or were they created in order to protect this knowledge from others? The T'ar-el were a multi-faceted species, and as such, Dar never doubted their powers—or how far across space they could wield them. No, Hamar didn't have an inkling. If he did, then the Sisterhood would know and deal with it, and him, accordingly.

Dar didn't want to waste precious time and energy berating himself for allowing this situation to happen. They had done the best they could, taken all measures known to them. Blame would never solve the equation; only skillful action would. He was just one man, although he had many at his side. Furthermore, he had a mission to complete and a personal promise to fulfill.

For a moment, Dar allowed himself to indulge memories of Galana and Bahar, especially Galana, whom he had held close against him, whose long slender hands he had grasped to his hearts at the end.

Hamar had poisoned them both. . .first figuratively, then literally, with his insistence that he would be the one to find the Waters of Nyr. After Bahar had died, Hamar's insistence had all but worn out Galana before he poisoned her as well. She had visited the Sisterhood too many times, lost too much blood. She'd been so depleted at the end, that her pale skin was nearly transparent, the dull blue of her veins all the more present.

What would Galana and Bahar say to him now? To the children they always longed for, but never knew would be born?

I will prepare Cassie now, Pree said without turning around as he murmured instructions to one of his assistants. Dar watched Pree begin the complex procedure to release Cassie from the healing pod. She looked so pale, deathly pale, and her mother's face filled his inner vision. But it was the circles beneath Cassie's eyes that disturbed Dar the most. The skin was bruised there in a most unsettling way, as if burned by what she saw within this Toori-induced nightmare.

As soon as Dar had realized the Toori had an energetic hold on Cassie, he'd told Pree to stop administering the sedative. Pree had complied at once, but the drug was still in her system, still holding her in a semi-comatose state, no doubt enhanced by some Toori meddling.

Several blue-suited guards remained at attention just beyond the doorway with orders to admit no one except for T'ai or Verson. Beneath the faint hum of the healing pod was an eerie silence. Most of the security detail was engaged in scouting the interior and exterior perimeters. Other personnel were preparing his ship for Ranat. He would have to leave a few staff behind to maintain the compound. Otherwise, Dar feared that Hamar would make sure the Toori would further infiltrate it.

Finished.

Dar heard Pree's voice within his mind and turned to look at Cassie, who was now lying on a mobile stretcher encased in a warming pod.

Have you been able to access her thoughts? Dar asked Pree, who lowered his head. *No.*

I hope she does not worsen when we leave. Pree said, studying Cassie for signs of waking, but there were none. It had been awhile since her last dose of sedative, but he didn't want to strain her system more by flushing out what remained.

You believe that will happen? Dar had wondered if moving Cassie would prove to be even more dangerous than allowing her to remain here.

I hope it will sever the Toori's hold. Our leaving.

Dar tapped his fingers, looking for a resolution to their current dilemma. Nothing appeared in his mind. T'ai and Verson were quite skilled with ferreting out signs of the Danyal imposter, or any Toori. Dar oscillated between hope-and-fear— that they would find the Toori spy and learn that it wasn't one of his trusted staff, that Hamar, with his Toori forces, hadn't succeeded in gaining complete control of Cassie's energetic stream, and that they were unable to apprehend Baron or any one else within their inner sanctum. Dar knew the situation would become worse before it returned to normal—whatever normal was.

Chapter 28

The starslips began to stir as Dar, Pree, and the medical attendants guiding Cassie's stretcher, entered the hangar.

Someone called out "Dar!" and he turned toward the familiar voice. Verson held up his muscled arm, circled his hand.

"We will ride with Verson and T'ai," Dar told Pree and the attendants. Cassie was still asleep, but there was a bit more color in her face, a sign that she was beginning to heal and would hopefully awaken soon.

Leaving is best, Pree said, resting a hand against Dar's chest to soothe him.

Dar nodded, and they maneuvered around the back of the hangar toward one of the middle starslips.

"We'll leave third. A bit of a buffer with the other two," Verson said.

Dar nodded his head, tapped his fingers together to focus his thoughts. "How long before we leave? Any sign of the Toori?"

"Not in the near vicinity. There is still some activity at the closed base, but no one has been seen leaving. They could be hiding in the north rock face." He paused checked his readouts again, took a deep breath. "Since Hamar has at least one device, they have an advantage."

"Let's hope they don't have any other advantages. At least we know the Toori was never in the same room with Cassie here on Poora. All Pree's assistants have been cleared."

"I would welcome tearing off its tentacles," Verson muttered under his breath.

There was a gust of cold air, and Dar and Verson turned toward its source, watched as the first starslip ascended vertically through the hangar, hovered, then slowly accelerated. Once it cleared the edges of the hangar's cover, the starslip spiraled into the sky until it was but a small blur in the dawn's pearl gray sky.

The next starslip began to hum, easing forward on the hangar's smooth stone surface to align with the hangar's opening.

"We are next," Verson said, grasping Dar's arm to assist him inside.

"Good journey," one of the ground crew called out as the starslip's petals closed in, encasing Dar, Verson, and their precious cargo.

"Good journey," Dar called back, hoping that nothing would befall the others left behind on Poora. He made sure everyone was situated, then sat down in his seat, closed his eyes, and called on the Four Corners for an insightful dream.

* * *

Soon after they left Poora's atmosphere, Cassie began to murmur in her sleep. Pree went to her side, laid a hand on her forehead. Her eyelids fluttered open and she looked around, struggled to sit up.

Please to lie down, Pree said in mindspeak, but she was insistent, so he helped her upright. One of his assistants had a container of water, which he handed to Pree.

"Please drink," he said, and she did.

"I had the most horrendous dream," she told everyone, rubbing her eyes, then brushing her hands through what she expected to be a tangled mess of hair. Someone had braided it close to her head, and she fingered the thin braids, smiled.

"It was not a dream," Dar said.

"I was afraid of that," she croaked out, reaching for the water, taking small sips even though she wanted to gulp it down.

"We are going to Ranat," Dar said in response to her noting the unusual surroundings."

"Baron?"

"He has gone on ahead. We were not sure if we could or should move you, then realized that we must. Baron, he had a similar dreamwalk, perhaps the same one. Take your time, but if you remember anything, anything at all. . ."

Cassie took another sip of water, smiled at Pree who purred, sat down next to her, pressing a hand to her back. It suffused her with so much warmth that she sighed, closed her eyes again, and slumped.

Pree started checking her vitals again.

"I'm okay. I'm okay. No headache, no feeling like I'm going to hurl, just achy all over, foggy, like I've been drugged or something. Just give me a few minutes to wake up. I'm not a morning person, you know." Cassie rubbed at her neck, attempted a smile.

"You know you had a seizure, correct?" Dar asked.

"I really was aware some of the time. I tried to wake up when I saw the Toori in my dream, but then Pree pumped me full of more drugs or something and whoosh, I was back there with those disgusting creatures."

"The sedation was for your own protection. The seizures. At first, we thought you had adverse effects to the trip here, then we discovered otherwise."

"That's never happened to me before. It was horrible, being tugged at like that."

"Could you be more specific?" Dar leaned forward.

"Like my insides were trying to come out. My body being turned inside out or splitting. It was really weird. First, I just started getting so cold, and my teeth started chattering and then it was out-of-control."

"Yes, we were very worried there for awhile. Pree here believed that leaving Poora might release their hold on you. I believe he was correct."

Cassie turned toward Pree. "Thank you for taking such good care of me. I felt safe with you, like my Grandmother was there, too."

"Your grandmothers are what you might call healers, too, Cassie. They had to be in order to carry and give birth to you."

"That would explain all those noxious teas, then." Cassie grimaced, then smiled. "And who braided my hair? I wish I had a mirror."

"Pree of the nimble hands," Dar said, nodding to Pree, who smiled, said, "Mahrainian style."

Cassie continued to finger the long braids, noticed there were beads woven throughout. She pulled a strand up to her eyes, examined the bead. "Is this coral? It's beautiful!"

Dar settled into a seat across from her. "What do you remember? Take it slow, as Pree here will not be pleased if I cause you more stress."

Pree glanced over at Dar, his large dark eyes luminous with concern.

"Well. Danyal is definitely not our brother. He lied. He's a Toori. I saw him change. Ugh. Are they like part octopus or something? Weird clammy folds of skin. Extra arms. I don't think they planned, or even wanted, to hurt me, but they were definitely threatening me—with what, I don't know. They were all cryptic, talked more to each other than to me. That Danyal thing said it wanted to show me something, and practically shoved me through this opening in a wall. That's when I woke up. But before, or at some point, I don't remember, I realized that they had some sort of force field thing around me. I remembered Ms. Brunhof, said I wanted to see her. She couldn't have totally hated us, could she? Like before she knew who we were, we really got along. She even put me and Baron together during class, then said something about how she should have done it earlier. I thought maybe I could reason with her, but they wouldn't let me. They said maybe later, if I, if we, Baron and I, cooperated, told them where the Waters of Nyr were." She paused, winded, coughed at the scratch in her throat, took another sip of water.

"I make tea," Pree said to Cassie, patting her on the shoulder. He stood, sent a "don't stress her" glance at Dar before making his way down the length of the starslip to a small cargo area. He searched through a variety of containers before he found the one he was looking for. He lifted the lid and pulled out an insulated bag with several large thermoses. He started to take out one of the thermoses, then slid it back into its protective casing, hefted the entire bag onto his left shoulder.

Pree walked back to where Dar and Cassie were sitting, pulled several small cups from the bag, set them gently down on a simple tray. He took out one of the thermoses, sniffed at its contents, then filled a cup, setting it carefully into Cassie's outstretched hands. He poured another for Dar, then one for himself.

A soothing floral scent permeated the ship. Cassie cupped her hands around the tea, bent her head to inhale its fragrance. "Hope it tastes as good as it smells."

Pree watched as she took her first sip, how her eyes widened with delight. "Mora Blossom tea. Very rare. Very good for you."

"It's great. I'll try not to gulp it down."

Dar was relieved to have Pree aboard. There wasn't anyone more qualified to care for Cassie, or anyone else on Poora and beyond, for that matter. He knew that Pree had genuine feelings for Cassie, cared for her in the same way that he had cared for Galana, Cassie's biological mother. How many times had Pree been at Galana's bedside during her short adult life? Through how many miscarriages? Then the death of Bahar, when she was mad with grief, and then at the end, with the virulent and gruesome poison that had taken her life?

Yes, it was good that Pree was here at Cassie's side. Perhaps some day he would attend the birth of Cassie's own child. Or Baron's and Ooli's.

Cassie said something Dar didn't hear. He'd been allowing his mind to wander. Galana and Bahar were no longer walking among them, but Cassie and Baron were. He needed to focus on them and their needs, and on the well-being of Mahrain.

"Please repeat that," he said, not sure if he'd heard the entire stream of words.

"The Toori that had been pretending to be Danyal—and how do they do that anyway? Well, it said that if we helped Uncle Hamar, we'd be left alone. I told the Toori that I didn't know what the Waters of Nyr were and neither did Baron, and then it said that there were ways to *make* us remember, that we did know. What could they do to us, Dar? What?"

Pree sent him a warning glance, which he acknowledged.

"Hamar of all people should know that remembering can *not* be forced. When we arrive at Ranat, there is someone who will help, someone who will guide you both to remember. It is possible that the mere act of wanting to remember will be enough. Or that deciding to remember will trigger the memories. As we say on Mahrain, nothing is ever truly forgotten. We only need to remember."

"I believe you, Dar. But if, I mean *when*, we remember, what's going to prevent Uncle Hamar from finding out, then doing whatever he plans to do with it?"

Remembering Pree's warning, all Dar said was, "We have our methods."

Chapter 29

The sun was just beginning to peer through the thick morning fog over the Mora Sea when the starslip pierced through Mahrain's atmosphere. While it descended, the starslip carrying Ooli and Baron morphed into a shape resembling the near extinct giant eel, Mahrain, for whom the planet was named. It dove deep into the frigid depths before leveling off to maneuver through the rock-strewn aquatic terrain, passing though several natural stone archways, which many believed belonged to the ruins of an ancient city that once thrived off the Mora coast.

Brilliant blue sea vines, iridescent pale green moss, and other aquatic plants clung to the piles of lava rock which partially obscured the passage. In the distance, several inactive volcanoes loomed, where small eels, fish, and other creatures made their home. Several scuttled or slithered away in the starslip's wake.

The membrane protecting Ooli and Baron released as the starslip eased around a curved rock sheath where they were met by the beacon lights of Ranat.

"Wow!" Baron said. "Wow. Just wow." "It's like an entire city beneath the ocean! Is it embedded in the rock?"

"Yeah. Partially natural, partially Mahrainian-made. That's sort of a joke. Remember I told you that Mahrain is the name for the giant eels that tunneled through here? And we're also Mahrainians. . ." She grinned, reached for a container of water, handed it to Baron. He opened it, took a long drink, wiped his mouth with the back of a hand.

"You see those two massive stones, that slight curve in the rock wall to the right?" She pointed, and Baron followed the length of her arm, nodded. "That's where we'll be pulling in. You'll feel some pressure when we dive and resurface. It usually takes most people a while to get acclimated here, which is one of the reasons Dar and Pree weren't sure about bringing Cassie, but I know they're close behind us."

Baron closed his eyes for a moment to think of his sister, to picture her in his mind, wish her a safe journey.

"You know, I feel that everything is going to be okay. I don't know why, but I just feel it's true." He pressed his hand against his chest, felt the subtle beating of his heart. "In here."

Ooli smiled, took several gulps of water. "That's the way to think. We have a saying on Mahrain. Believe, and then allow it to happen. It might lose a bit in translation, but that's basically it."

"We have the same on Haura—either that, or it's part of my Grams' philosophy." He ran a hand through his tangled hair, wished he'd done a better job of tying it back before they left.

Ooli tugged out her hair ties, massaged her scalp, wondered how long before she'd get to take a nice hot soak in a mineral bath. It felt good to be home, and she hoped that Baron and Cassie, once all the madness was over, would be happy here. Returning to Haura wouldn't be an option for them. Not for a long time, if ever. The subject hadn't been raised, but she couldn't help but wonder if they realized the reality of their situation. Did they think their only purpose was to find the Waters of Nyr? That once found, they would return to normal lives on Haura?

Ooli would miss Haura, too, but one of the main reasons she loved being there was sitting right next to her, the other, in a starslip close behind.

"Cassie says we need to learn Mahrainian, but I'm not that good at languages." Baron's voice trailed off as he was pressed backward in his seat. The starslip dove, wended around several stone columns, then breached the water's surface. It glided across the wide expanse of a natural pool toward an embankment, where there were several men waiting.

"Hold on!" Ooli called out, reaching for Baron's hands as he stood up and tried to clamber over her. "It might morph again before it lets us out."

"Before it lets us? You never did tell me just what this ship is made out of."

"No, I guess I didn't. You were too busy stargazing. Do you remember any of what I told you?"

Eyebrows raised, he shook his head. "I can't remember the names of all those moons, but I do remember that Poochi Bug thing. Some constellation that looks like a Poochi Bug. Any of them here?"

"Not at Ranat, but on the surface. We do have other creatures to deal with. Mostly benign. Some not so much. You really will be debriefed this time, but it is an ongoing process. Back on Poora, there just wasn't time. Besides, new planet, new terrain, new rules."

Baron looked down at Ooli's hands surrounding his. While he didn't want her to let go, he felt the urge to hold her hand in his rather than the other way around. True, his hands weren't much larger than Ooli's, but hers were definitely stronger. He was almost getting up the nerve to switch hand positions when the right side of the starslip began to undulate.

"Well, it looks like it's going to let us get out before returning to its pod form."

An opening appeared in the side of the starslip, and a ramp unfurled where Baron hadn't even noticed there was a door, much less a ramp rolled up somewhere. One of the men on the embankment stepped onto the ramp, took a few steps toward the interior of the craft, reached in to assist Ooli, then Baron, out onto the embankment.

"Welcome to Ranat, Baran. Nice to see you again, Ooli." the man said in English, and Baron, who noticed the different pronunciation of his name, wondered if this was the way his name was supposed to be pronounced. Then it dawned on him that with so many of these aliens speaking English, maybe learning Mahrainian might not be absolutely necessary. He paused. Alien. He was an alien, too, it seemed—and so was Cassie and Ooli. It hadn't quite sunk in yet.

None of them were human—or were they?

Baron wished he was better with mindspeak so he could talk to Ooli without the others hearing. Then again, they were probably Mahrainian and would hear them anyway. If he had to venture an educated guess, Baron realized that Mahrainians were tall by Hauran standards. But how was he supposed to be able to tell who was from what planet or species what with all this shape-shifting stuff and synthsuits? Furthermore, he was certain that this wasn't all he and Cassie were going to have to deal with. If he'd only known he'd need his supposed gifts to survive on another world, he might have encouraged his Grams more.

"Thank you," Baron said, reaching out to shake the man's hand. Ooli clasped it instead, and the man seemed to be none the wiser. Baron realized that he had no idea what was polite and rude in his new culture, his new world. On the positive side, though, this was the first time he felt relaxed enough to even begin thinking about being polite for quite some time.

"I'm Ooli," she said to one of the men she didn't recognize, bowing slightly.

"Ah, yes, formal introductions. I am Jenar, your—" he paused, not sure about the word to describe his function, or whether now was the right time to share this information.

"I am Jenar," he repeated, then actually smiled, which relaxed Baron even more.

"This," he said pointing at one of the three other men," is Taral. He is brother to T'ai, who you know. Then this," he clasped the other man's shoulder," is my brother, Rane. And this is Dari, no relation to the person you know as Dar, Ooli's **bua**."

Baron nodded and smiled directly at each one, his hand still firmly grasped inside Ooli's. He heard the word, bua, wondered what it meant. Were Dar and Ooli married or something? He wondered about that possibility for a brief moment, then realized that it must mean boss or something like that.

"Please follow us. There is refreshment and others to greet you. Then we will begin with a short tour of our facilities with cautionary information about indigenous life forms you may encounter while here. I assure you, though, Ranat is safe from the Toori—" Jenar paused before continuing, and Baron hoped that he hadn't been about to list who—or what—he wouldn't be safe from here.

With Jenar leading, Taral, Rane, and Dari surrounded Baron and Ooli as they walked across the cave floor. More of the guarding bit, Baron noted, then tried not to get agitated. They were safe on Ranat now, and that was all that mattered.

It was a bit chilly, but not as cold as Baron anticipated after the initial blast of cold air when they'd climbed out of the starslip. He sniffed and noticed the usual ocean scents, but there was an underlying sweetness, as if flowers were blooming somewhere. It was an intoxicating scent, and he wanted to find the source of the perfume. It reminded him a bit of night blooming jasmine, which was a welcome nostalgic scent.

Baron looked around the grotto, but didn't see any floating flowers. Just the starslip with a few strands of sea grass or kelp attached to its surface, which had morphed into what Ooli said was its natural pod shape. He remembered visiting Balboa Park's lily pond a few times with his Grams. She was always painting that pond, and was totally bummed when they took all the koi and water lilies out. He remembered reading about several aquatic flowers that smelled awesome, but how could you smell them under water?

But this wasn't Balboa Park, and he wasn't in San Diego anymore. He wasn't even on Earth—or Haura. He was in an underwater city, an aquatic space station, surrounded by and constructed of rocks and caves and who knew what else. Just to his right, the wall was pitted with openings large enough for a man of his size—or larger—to wriggle through. He peered closer, wondered if there were flowers blooming further inside the tunnels that traveled through the porous rock.

"What are those?" he whispered to Ooli. "They look like snake holes or something." He shuddered, imagining huge snakes—or worse—slithering out and dropping on them. In fact, he realized, turning as best as he could since as he was practically corralled by the other men, that this area reminded him of a huge pit rather than a cave.

"Actually, they are," she whispered back.

Without breaking stride or turning around, Jenar said, "But the sea snakes, the *Mahrain,* that made them are gone. We made sure of it. If there are any left in the vicinity, they won't be able to breach the facility except through this area. We keep watch."

Baron could hear what he translated as laughter in his mind, along with the words, "good eating," and he wondered if the eels or he would be the meal. He realized they were just playing with him, and this further lightened his mood, the major stress of the past few days drifting away.

There was a series of steps ahead that led up to what at first appeared to be a dead end. Baron stepped up and peered around, saw how there was a sharp turn, and the stairwell spiraled up through the cave. They climbed these, with Jenar still leading. After several flights of stairs, Baron began to feel a bit winded and his ears were beginning to pop. Nausea was creeping into his throat, and he thought of Cassie and her sensitive stomach. Baron stopped to catch his breath, leaned against the cool rock face.

"How much further?" he panted, and made a mental note to find the Mahrainian equivalent of a gym. He was totally out-of-shape.

"Please excuse me for rushing you, Baran," Jenar said extending his arms palms up, "but we are all eager to see you both inside to prepare for the next transport. I believe your sister, Casaya, will be aboard one of the next few slips with Dar and Pree."

"Come on," Ooli said, "I'll give you a hand." Then she practically drug him up the next series of steps which finally opened up onto somewhat level ground. After walking up a slight incline and passing through a short corridor, they entered an area bustling with activity.

There were a few solitary individuals as well as several groups of people walking this way and that, most of them dressed in a style that would blend in on Haura without even the turn of a head. A few were wearing the loose-fitting clothes from Poora. Others wore various styles and colors of skin-tight suits that reminded him of scuba divers. Mostly shades of blue and green, while some seemed to be faceted, as their color changed as they moved. They all looked human, more or less, which surprised Baron, as he had prepared himself for more strange sights along the lines of the Toori—or worse.

Ooli tugged him along. They turned left then right around a

curved wall and Baron stopped in his tracks. He took a step back, then another. On the opposite side of the spacious well-lit area was a transparent wall, and behind it, the most humongous aquarium he had ever seen. Some of the fish looked just like the ones he'd seen on Haura, but others looked like something out of a xenophobic nightmare. One in particular had its gills pressed against the glass, its tentacles fluttering around as if it were trying to find a doorknob or some other way to breach the wall.

"Who's in the aquarium—them or us?" He exhaled his pent-up air, took a step closer.

"Advanced technology and a bit of Mahrainian magic," she grinned, then pointed toward a squat bulbous creature that shuffled toward them. It paused, then unfurled brilliant blue tendrils that undulated around its head. Each tendril ended in a small iridescent globe. "You want to watch out for that sucker. It's called a *toola*, and can eat a whole Mahrainian."

His almond-shaped eyes widened further. "Seriously?"

"Seriously," Jenar replied. "It is beautiful, isn't it? It looks similar to your anemone, but it doesn't adhere to any one surface. It can move through the water. They prefer to camouflage themselves with sea grass to catch unsuspecting fish and whatnot.

They don't actually eat you whole, but take small bites, or dissolve you, over an extended period of time. Fortunately, they numb you first with their poisonous barbs. We have a great respect for the sea on Mahrain as some do on Haura as well. We also refer to the sea as female. A nice similarity, no?"

Ooli managed to guide Baron along with the assistance of the others. After they passed through the glass-walled room separating them from the Mora Sea, they turned into a small alcove that opened up into a comfortable rest area. It almost looked like a living room or den back on Haura, Baron thought, and then he saw them!

"Grams!" He ran, picked her up, and circled around. "Cassie's Grams!" And then he repeated the process, grabbed them both, hugged them over and over again, and didn't even wipe away the tears cascading down his cheeks. Finally, he squeezed them each one more time, pressed his lips on top of their well-coiffed heads.

"Whoa," he said. "I think I've grown a few inches."

"Cassie?" Gramma Iliana asked, looking from Baron to Ooli back to Baron and then to Jenar.

"Next transport," Jenar said, then bowed out of the room along with the others, leaving Baron and Ooli alone with Iliana and Selene.

Chapter 30

"Let me look at you," Baron's Gramma Selene said, holding him at arm's length. "Yes, you have grown taller. Quite a bit. . .but so thin. We'll fix that," she said, winking at Iliana, who was perched on the edge of one of the plush green cushions that could easily pass for a Hauran sofa.

"And your hair—so long now." She caressed the unruly mass of thick black hair that now tumbled over his shoulders and down his back.

"Let's have some cocoa—and with just the right amount of cinnamon, of course, as I made it myself," Iliana said, lifting a metal pot from its warmers and pouring the steaming chocolate into four large cups.

Baron sighed with delight, leaned forward to reach for his cup, hold it between his two hands. He relished the moment, as it was suffused with the first signs of home that Baron had experienced outside his memories in months.

"Ummm," Ooli sighed. "I would love some." She plopped down on the sofa next to Iliana and waited for her cup, which she held reverently between her hands, leaning forward to inhale its pungent bittersweet fragrance.

"Careful, sweetie. It's hot," Iliana said, resting a hand along her cheek. "And haven't you grown up to be a beauty—and a starslip pilot as well."

"Why am I not surprised you two know each other," Baron said, sitting down next to his Grams on the sofa, then setting the cup down on the low table in front of him.

"Of course we do, sweetie. Ooli is Dar's daughter. We've known her since before she was born, you could say."

"Figures," he said, studying her face for signs of Dar. "I was wondering what was up with you two." He studied her face like the artist he was. The word, "beautiful", came into his mind. *Yes, beautiful.* He cocked his head to the side to study her high cheekbones, the slight slant of her eyes, her lovely mouth. "You must look like your mother."

Ooli grinned, leaned against Iliana who circled an arm around her shoulders for a hug. "Yes, that's what I've been told, but I suppose I look like both of my parents. A little bit of each. I haven't seen her for a long time, though. She moved away when I little."

"I'm sorry," Baron said.

"Don't be." She smiled, tapped her forehead. "I carry her image with me wherever I go."

While they sipped their cocoa, Baron gazed at his Grams, Iliana, and Ooli. The people he loved. He noticed how both the Grammsies wore their silver hair in an intricate series of braids now, and their usual slacks or jeans and loose-fitting tops had been replaced with those pajama clothes Mahrainians seemed to favor. His Grams's was a pale lilac, and Cassie's Grams, a soft shade of green. Jade, he believed it was called. Yes, Jade green. He also noticed that they looked remarkably young, despite their silver hair, to be grandmothers. . .How could they look younger than the last time he'd seen them? He shrugged off the impossibility of this and figured it must be because they were safe and happy to see him.

And then he remembered how they were Cassie's and his birth mothers, so if he had to guess, he doubted they were even forty. Their age didn't matter to him, but he wondered how old Ooli was, and that if she were a lot older, would she think he was just a kid. Was he supposed to call his Grams "mother" now? He knew that he could if she asked him to.

No one's age mattered right now. What mattered was that everyone appeared healthy and happy. Cassie was on her way, and they would be a family again. They were long overdue for this reunion.

"So what happened?" Baron began, looking from his Grams to Cassie's, and back again. "What happened that day you disappeared?"

"I suppose we really should fill you in now. Selene?" Iliana set her cup down, turned to her life-long friend.

"That day will forever be emblazoned in my mind," Selene began, settling back against a plush cushion. "Iliana and I had just been at the market. We were rushing a bit as we were supposed to be meeting with Dar at Iliana's house. Iliana was putting the grocery bags in the back of her car while I fumbled with the car keys and dropped them into one of the bags."

"If you hadn't been so clumsy, we might not have seen them," Iliana added.

"Seen who?" Baron asked, leading forward, knowing the answer.

"Toori," Selene said with disgust. "Oh, they were disguised, but I knew them right away."

Iliana nodded. "Their synthsuits didn't fit quite right. A dead give-away—plus that smell." She rubbed at her nose.

"I never noticed Ms. Brunhof smell bad," Baron mused.

"You're just not sensitized to it yet. When Toori are in their natural form, it's really difficult to tell them apart. But the scent gives the males away. Some sort of musk.

I can see why you wouldn't smell Ms. Brunhof, who, by the way, was with them that day. They tried to act all nonchalant as they walked toward us across the parking lot, as if they were just on the way to their own car. The parking lot was pretty full, and there was that nice young man who offered to help us out to the car retrieving carts."

She paused, tapped her fingers together. "There were four of them. Yes. Three males and Ms. Brunhof. I remember what she looked like from the time I visited your class. I should have known she was Toori then, but as I said before, it's the males that release that odor, not the females."

"So what did you do? What happened?" Ooli asked. "I haven't heard all the details yet."

"We got out of there in a hurry," Iliana added, chuckling. "You should have seen her drive! How do you kids say it? Like a bat out of hell?" She smiled, shook her head.

"We shoved the groceries in the backseat, locked all the doors, strapped in, then tore out of that parking lot. I'm glad there weren't any police, as I would have gotten a ticket for sure, and who knows what the Toori would have done. . .even in broad daylight.

So, there must have been a van idling for them, as it didn't take long before they clambered into it and followed us. We managed to lose them for a bit, but then they found us again. This happened several times, so either they know the streets better than we do, which is possible, or they had some sort of tracking device, which is much more likely.

We didn't want to lead them back to the house—to either of our houses—in case you and Cassie were there, so we kept circling around, hoping to confuse them." Selene was quiet for a moment. Vivid imagery reeled through her mind so fast that it all became a blur.

Iliana patted Selene's hand, continuing. "I think we parked the car over by that other market, you know the one that sells the Mexican chocolate, then ran up the alley to the back of that video rental place you go. The Four Corners. As you've pro-bably guessed now, it's one of ours. There's a safe house there, too. Jenar was there, but hadn't opened the store yet. He heard us coming," Iliana took Ooli's hand, stroked the top of it.

"Yeah. Thank the Four Corners for mindspeak! Jenar said it was more like mindyelling, though," Ooli grinned. "Jenar, you just met him, remember? FYI, he's the one that usually makes those ooey-gooey lemon bars you like, Baron. So be sure to stay on his good side and he may just whip you up a batch. He's quite the chef when he's not squelching Toori."

"And then what happened?" Baron asked, leaning forward to pour himself more cocoa.

Ooli took a sip from her cup, then another. "Well, let's see," she said. "Too bad Jenar's not back to fill you in on the tech stuff. I was at The Star Gazer. We knew there'd been a sighting by the time you and Cassie showed up. Verson was waiting for you two there, primed to respond, if need be."

"That was the day we were going to tell you two the truth," Selene interrupted. Iliana and I were going to meet with Dar first. Then, when you and Cassie got home from school, we were going to introduce you. . ." her voice trailed off, and she closed her eyes, sighed.

Selene rubbed at her eyes, brushed a stray lock of her hair behind an ear. "Jenar took us down to the basement—it's fortified—to wait, contacted another one of the safe houses to prepare for transport. We didn't get a chance to contact Dar right away, which I regret, but everything happened so fast, and we were afraid of being intercepted. We knew Dar would let himself into Iliana's if we weren't there. Then—"

Selene continued. "Then Jenar and Tari, was it?" She looked at Iliana, who nodded. "Yes, then Jenar sent Tari and three of their team out to look for the Toori. Apparently, they'd found Iliana's car. One of the Toori was rummaging around beneath the hood, tearing out plugs and hoses. Another was rummaging through the back seat. I don't know what they thought they'd find, it was just groceries, but Tari managed to down that one, then two others came out of nowhere and blasted at Tari." She took a deep breath, exhaled, then murmured, "Thank the Four Corners they missed."

Ooli set down her cup, zig-zagged her long hands through the air. "They have one of our transport devices, and that Ms. Brunhof grabbed the dead one and disappeared in the proverbial flash of green before Tari could grab her. The other ones managed to hide somewhere for awhile. I didn't hear whether they turned up or not. Jenar would know."

Ooli looked toward the door, cocked her head to listen for sounds of Jenar, or one of his men, with news of the other starslip arrivals. "They usually travel in groups of at least three," she said, "as one of their few admirable qualities is that they don't leave their own behind. Can you imagine if a Toori were to get captured on Haura?" She asked Baron.

"Yeah, the powers that be would have had a field day. News at 11 and all that stuff. Government cover-ups, conspiracies. You name it." He shook his head, thought about saying a few more things, decided against it, returned to sipping his cocoa and listening to Ooli.

"We didn't contact my *bua*, I mean, Dar, until later in the day until after the one came after you and Cassie. Verson was there, fortunately. There was another man in the back kitchen, too. Rane, Jenar's little brother. We usually had a least two of our team there all the time. Besides me. But I'm not trained to fight, really. I have other skills. . ." Ooli looked into Baron's eyes for a moment, just a moment, and he felt a hot wind circle around in his chest. He took a deep breath, coughed.

"You okay, sweetie?" His Grams stroked his back. He nodded, cleared his throat, and Ooli continued.

"After that, there were still a few people at the café, so when I realized what was up, I closed the café down. Told people we had a family emergency and had to close the café and didn't know when we'd open again. There was a bit of grumbling, but I gave everyone bags of pastries—didn't want them to go to waste."

"We were so worried about you and Cassie, hoped that you'd do the smart thing and head to Iliana's, which, Thank the Four Corners, you did." Selene reached out to hug Baron, held him close against her, and began to sob quietly against his shoulder.

"This is not what we wanted, sweetie. Those Toori, at least they didn't get their dirty hands on you." She wiped her tears with the back of a sleeve.

"There, there, Grams," he hugged her back. "It's okay. Cassie and I are safe now. She's on her way, and we'll all be together again."

"You're a good boy," she said, "I mean, man." She hesitated, brightened, looked deep within his obsidian eyes. "I'm proud to have been your *mua*, your mother. I so wish that your true mother had lived to see you become a man."

"Thank you, Grams. I wish I'd met her, too, but for the record, whenever I think of my mother, it's *your* face I see in my mind." He hugged her again, and felt her relax against him, not wanting to let go of her or her of him.

"I wonder how much longer before Cassie and Dar are here. . ." Iliana sighed, looked at Ooli to respond.

"They were staggering the ships. Dar—" and then she turned to Baron, "I feel like I should use his formal name to talk about all this. . .Since we all know each other, I suppose I can call him *bua* in front of you now, our word for father. You'll pick up on Mahrainian in a heartbeat, Baron. Trust me. Okay, bua said they'd be coming on the third or fourth starslip. Just in case. Before nightfall, hopefully." She squeezed Iliana's hand.

"So where'd you go, Grams?" Baron reached for her cup, handed it to her. She took a sit, cradled it in her hands.

"We stayed at The Four Corners for most of the day. We have a few other buildings with starslip hangars in San Diego, and several others in nearby states. Yes, Arizona," she smiled. "So, Jenar alerted them and we waited for transport. It took several weeks before we left Haura, though. We came directly here to Mahrain, to Ranat, although we wanted to join you on Poora." She grimaced, and her pale blue eyes turned steel gray. "Hamar," she nearly spat, "may he be slowly devoured by a Nara, contacted us en route."

"Ah yes, Uncle Hamar. Dar told me about him. Did you see him?"

"Only on what you'd probably call a vidscreen, fortunately. But he made it clear he knew you and Cassie were on Poora and that he was going to get what he wanted."

Baron stood up from the couch, began to pace around the room. "The Waters of Nyr. The Waters of Nyr—what are they, Grams? Cassie and I have no idea—and why is Uncle Hamar so bent on getting them?"

Iliana and Selene exchanged a glance. "We will both tell and show you when Cassie arrives. Certainly not today. After you both rest for awhile. You need to be prepared—" Baron cut her off.

"You mean you know where they are? It's not a mystery?" Baron was so surprised that he was practically yelling, and at his beloved Grams. "I'm sorry, " he said, hanging his head. "I didn't mean to yell, but I thought they were hidden and we had to find them."

"You've carried them all along, sweetie," Selene began. "You and Cassie both. It's an ability. The waters themselves are part of the process, I suppose you'd say. One of the Sisterhood will come to assist you, and then we will see what we will see."

Chapter 31

It was early afternoon on Mahrain, and Baron was awakened by intense natural light filtering through his sleeping quarters from a skylight embedded in the vaulted ceiling above his bed. It felt wondrous to feel the sun on his face after being cooped up on Poora, and he could hardly wait to venture above to feel it directly on his skin.

Baron! Cassie spoke in his mind.

He sat bolt-upright in bed, tossed off the covers, looked around the room.

I'm next door. You slept the day away snorting like a suckling pig. And then she laughed!

I'll be right there—but where is there?

I'll be there in a sec.

Baron yawned, stretched, then pulled on a shirt that was draped over a stool by his bed. He went into the bathroom to splash cold water on his face, ran his hands through the tangled mess of his black curly hair. He'd been so tired after talking with Cassie and the Grammsies, Ooli, Dar, and Jenar until all hours. The night before was a blur that undulated through his mind, never quite taking solid shape. He didn't even remember going to bed, and hoped that he hadn't fallen asleep on the couch and been carried in here by Jenar—or worse, Ooli.

Within a few minutes, the door to his room slid open, and there was Cassie with Ooli and the Grammsies.

"It's too late for breakfast, so you'll have to wait until dinner. Here's a snack," Ooli said with a grin, clearly holding something behind her back. Baron reached around her, and she side-stepped away from him, then held the bowl out.

"No way! You have ooey-gooey lemon bars."

"Way!" she said, handing him the bowl with a playful ceremonious bow. "You need to thank Jenar, though. Our citrus fruit isn't the same as yours, but I guarantee you'll love these."

Baron started to reach out for one, then pulled his hand back to grab Cassie with both arms. They hugged for a long time, then rocked each other back-and-forth. "I missed you, little sister. I thought I only dreamt you were here."

"Must have been some nightmare," she giggled liked her old self.

"Hey—I'm older, aren't I, Gramma?"

Iliana just shrugged. "Twins you're not, but you were born the same day. . ." her voice trailed off.

Selene chuckled. "We actually had you at home. Back then," and she looked wistful, "Iliana and I lived in the same house. We planned to raise you together, but unfortunately, we weren't able to." A tear slid from her eye. "No sense in focusing on the past. . .We're together now."

"So, you're okay?" Baron asked, extending a hand toward Ooli for the lemon bars. He offered one to Cassie, who shook her head, extended the plate all around the room, but no one else wanted one. He shrugged, took a huge bite, sighed with ecstasy.

"Tell Jenar I'll be his BFF," Baron mumbled through a mouthful of cookie.

"BFF?" Selene asked.

"Best Friends Forever," Ooli replied. "Geekspeak."

"Ah," Selene responded. "Well, bring your bowl—and slip into those sandals. We have a lot to see, even more to discuss before a walk, and perhaps dinner, on the surface, weather willing."

* * *

Jenar arrived to lead them on a short tour. Baron's first assessment, that Ranat was like an entire city underwater, was only partially correct. While it was self-sustaining and approximately five-hundred people both lived and worked there, Ranat was not open to the general populace. Its official purpose was that of an aquatic research and development facility which provided natural, as well as Mahrainian-made, sanctuaries. Its unofficial purposes were many, and included providing a safe haven for those in need of refuge.

The primary facility wended around the coastline of the Mora Sea, then jutted out to provide easier access to their deep-sea modules. Two domed sections extended above Mahrain's surface which provided land access and contained meeting rooms, living, and guest quarters.

"It's more or less summer now, on Mahrain," Jenar said to Cassie and Baron. "The weather is much like your San Diego's July gloom. Or is it June gloom? I forget. Anyway, Ranat is obviously on the ocean, or seaside, of Mahrain. We have several smaller oceans or seas—I never can figure out the difference between those two on Haura. So, we have many islands. Volcanoes, mostly extinct, except for an occasional eruption near the steppes. That's Poochi territory, too. They thrive there with the warm soil. Burrowers. Their honey, exquisite." He smacked his lips.

"I saw the Poochi Bug constellation on the way here," Baron said, glancing at Ooli, walking next to him so close that he could just extend his fingers to touch her hand as it swung gracefully as she walked.

"Hopefully, you will have an opportunity to visit the hives soon. They're quite fascinating creatures," he grinned.

"No thank you," Baron said.

"Then no honey for you," Ooli playfully thumped him on the arm, to which he responded with a loud "youch!"

"We just left one of several residential areas in this wing. Each has its own lounge area, too. This isn't a vacation resort, you know, so there's quite a bit going on at any given time. First arrivals are ushered in from a variety of the landing pools, so it's a busy zone, depending upon whether or not people are coming in via starslip.

There are other means of access to Ranat," he continued, quickening his pace, "both from the water and above. We're coming toward the aquatic center, now, which is really just a long hallway from one section to another. That's the way we came in when you arrived.

"Up ahead are some dining areas, bathing facilities, and I suppose you would call them water locks where our divers go down. Some prefer to swim to other parts of Ranat rather than walk or climb the stairs. We have observation stations strewn throughout the area. Some aren't connected."

"Where's all the high tech stuff?" Baron asked, expecting to see much more signs of that.

"What do you study here?" Cassie asked.

Jenar didn't respond to Baron's question, but did to Cassie's. "The usual thing. Aquatic life. Bioengineering. He turned to Baron. "Are you up for a bit of a climb?"

"He should be. He slept all day," Cassie said, laughing.

"Someone feels better than okay," Baron groaned. "You could have woke me up!' He shook his head, said, "Sure, Jenar," then looked ahead at the narrow ramp that led up along the side of a rock wall. There were grooves carved into either side, and Baron slid his fingers between them. He thought that they might be some sort of handrail, but if so, what manner of hand would be able to grip them? At the end of the ramp, there was the first set of steps carved out of the rock and reinforced with a spongy material that gripped his sandals, making the climb considerably easier.

"I'll give you a shove," Ooli said, and Baron took the stairs two or three at a time to catch up with Jenar, who turned around, a look of concern on his face.

"Casaya—are you sure that this isn't too much for you?"

"No, I'm fine. And I love the way you pronounce my name. Is that the Mahrainian pronunciation?"

"Yes, it is. Your names were given a Hauran twist, but we have always referred to you as Casaya and Baran." Satisfied that Casaya wasn't getting winded, he continued up the steep stairwell, then paused at an intersection.

"What's up there?" Cassie pointed to the left pathway, then rested for a moment, leaning against the smooth rock wall. She was surprised that the moist air didn't reek of damp.

"Fresh air, for one," Jenar smiled. "After you, Baran."

While Baron was definitely short of breath when they reached the top of the stairwell, it was well worth it. He closed his eyes, extended his arms and just breathed in the warm air. The sun was out, but thankfully not too hot. When he opened his eyes again, he gasped. There, looming practically above them, were two of Mahrain's moons.

"Oh my—" Baron tilted his head back further, nearly loosing his balance. Ooli gave him a little push to restore his footing.

"No, they won't fall on you, silly," she said.

"Where's the third moon, Jenar?" Cassie walked sideways, then back again, on the pebbled surface.

"You can't see Soola from here very well. At night, though, you will be able to. While it's larger than Bejar, which is that moon, there," Jenar pointed to the moon on the far left that appeared to be sinking into the Mora Sea, "it's further out, and visibility varies. Sometimes, it has a red tinge around it at night. I'll take you to our observatory soon. It's quite spectacular."

"It's where I will be living," Cassie said in her usual matter-of-fact way, and then paused to wonder at how easily she had become emotionally and mentally acclimated to traveling from one planet to another.

Iliana looked as if she'd been slapped. "What did you say, sweetie?"

Cassie saw how upset her grandmother was, and wondered why. But there was that old fear in her grandmother's eyes. Fear and something else that she wasn't sure how to define.

"It just fell out of my mouth, Gramma."

Iliana closed her eyes, said a silent prayer to the Four Corners. She rested her hands against her stomach, pressed, remembering when Cassie first quickened inside her. Her baby, her *tua* Cassie, no, her Casaya, was destined for the Sisterhood? How could this be? No, it couldn't be true. She was just going to visit, live there for a time. Not the Sisterhood. She wanted her here, by her side, living as normal a life as possible.

Iliana exchanged glances with Selene, who then closed her eyes to communicate with mindspeak. *Only time will tell if that is her path, sister.*

"I'm sorry to get so upset and spoil our lovely outing, but there are things about that planet, things that I hope you never need to do, never experience, my Casaya."

They hugged, and Cassie murmured. "It's okay, Gramma. I'll be back. I won't stay forever."

She felt her grandmother, who she now knew was her mua, relax against her. "Yes," she said, "in the way that you know things, in the way that I know them, too. I will come with you, then."

Cassie and Iliana rested their foreheads against each other, and Cassie couldn't remember the last time they had done that, not since she was a little girl plagued with strange dreams and nightmares that she now knew were visions of another world, another life.

Chapter 32

The next morning, everyone was awakened before first light. At first, they thought it was just for an early breakfast before an outing on Mahrain's surface or some other activity at Ranat. It didn't take long for Cassie and Baron to realize that something seriously bad had happened. Dar didn't look like he had slept at all, his dark, deep-set eyes struggling to remain open, his jaw clenched tight.

"I have distressing news," he said, and all eyes were on him.

"The Poora station was attacked by Toori. They waited until the last starslip left before descending upon it en masse. Apparently, they read our departure as a decoy, that we were still at P1."

Is everyone okay, Ooli mindspoke to her bua, Dar, but knew the answer without his response.

"These were not ordinary Toori. Another clan from the mining colony, Psion IV, no doubt. Kham miners built of sturdier stock. They exist in horrendous conditions—even thrive there it seems." He paused, locked eyes with Jenar, said, "Hamar was with them."

Jenar spoke first.

"Then he's probably deduced we're on Mahrain. Has he even been to Ranat? Does he know it's operational?"

Dar nodded.

Baron looked from Dar to Jenar. "Did anyone survive? Weren't there still a few starslips left behind?"

Dar shook his head. "We are not absolutely sure, but it does not appear so. The station was ransacked, and the shells, May They Journey Beyond The Four Corners, of thirteen of our people were found. A few are still unaccounted for, but fortunately, Hamar didn't kill Nal. He had to leave someone behind to—how do you say, tell the tale?"

Jenar nodded, closed his eyes. He had several friends back on Poora, and called out to the Four Corners to protect and grant them a speedy rebirth on a higher plane.

"There was a message from Hamar which I will not translate in full at the moment. Essentially, he has announced that he is returning for a visit to his family home on Mahrain and requests a meeting with us here at Ranat. It is likely he will arrive in an official Trilune vessel under the pretense of an official visit. We will play that game, deal with him accordingly."

“Sozar! He’s not even fit for a nara meal,” Iliana said, her eyes steel gray with anger and determination. “Perhaps we can set a little trap for him.”

All eyes were on Iliana now, but Baron and Cassie were shocked to see how her face had transformed. Gone was Cassie’s sweet grandmother, their mua. In her place was a woman of power who emanated palpable energy.

Baron shuddered, looking from Iliana to Selene, realizing that her face was also set in a fierce mask of determination. And then it dawned on him. Their Grammsies would have to be strong women to survive all that they had thus far. And to protect him and Cassie.

“What can I, what can *we*, do?” Baron asked with more confidence than he felt. He wanted to, had to, do something to help. All this effort for them? It had to mean something—and why did they deserve the dedication and protection of all these people? Just for being who they were? No! He yelled inside his mind. We need to deserve it. We need to repay the debt.

Yes we do, Cassie agreed. She, too, had noticed their grandmothers’—no, their mothers’—shift in energy, and felt it rise within her as well.

Jenar glanced at Baron, heard him thrash about in his mind to find meaning, to figure out some sort of action. He cleared his throat. “Why don’t we organize a little welcome ceremony, be gracious hosts as a measure of good will. It will create time to for us to figure out how to proceed next.” He grinned, and it wasn’t a pleasant sight. “We’ll just offer him what the Haurans refer to as diplomatic immunity.”

“And then what?” Baron asked, feeling Ooli’s hand as it moved to cover his, radiating heat and pulsing with unreleased energy. She, too, was fierce, and he was learning that the females of Mahrain were a force of nature—and if possible, something even more profound. But what effect would it have on his poor excuse for an uncle, Hamar, and his Toori hit men, or whatever they were?

“We will show him the Waters of Nyr,” Cassie said, her eyes glistening.

“Okay,” Baron said, looking from Cassie to Iliana and Selene, then pausing for a moment to study the other men’s faces before he turned to Ooli. “Just tell me what to do.”

Chapter 33

It was mid-morning on Mahrain. A dense natural fog blocked out the sun's tentative rays, barely illuminating the Trilune ship carrying Hamar, which hovered while awaiting permission to land at Ranat.

Jenar kept him waiting.

Once cleared, Hamar, along with two official aides, completed their journey to the surface in a small cruiser. Jenar, Dar, Verson, and several security staff, watched as the pilot maneuvered deftly through the thick fog, just clearing a lagoon as it landed on a small patch of unclaimed solid ground.

After consulting with Dar, Jenar had designated this landing area on purpose, as it was rarely used except for an alternate access to the massive aquarium. Located on the east side of Ranat, it would be easier to control the situation should Hamar violate their agreement. It would also be easier to manage his comings-and-goings to the official vessel.

If he were allowed to leave.

When the station was under construction, it had also been a well-used entrance to the lower caverns and caves. Several caretakers had lived and worked within its confines, and the live-work spaces had been maintained for visiting scientists as well as other personnel.

The cruiser was on the ground for several minutes before an exit ramp slid open. Hamar took a few tentative steps down the steep metal ramp, paused to study the official greeting party, then resumed his descent accompanied by two aides. As soon as the three men cleared the ramp, it recoiled back into the cruiser. Without further delay, the craft rose vertically into the fog, returning to the Trilune vessel.

That's an intriguing development, Jenar mindspoke to Dar.

Indeed, Dar replied. *I expected the cruiser to remain here as well. I wonder what he believes this will prove.*

As was customary, they waited for their guest to speak first.

"Thank you for extending us the courtesy of an official visit," Hamar said, bowing slightly.

He appeared much older, Dar thought, noticing how Hamar's blue-black hair was now streaked with silver, that the skin seemed looser around those eerie blue eyes. Despite the outward signs of age, however, Dar noticed that the man was still fit, his official blue-gray

Trilune uniform clinging to his large well-developed frame. Trilune's insignia was evident on his chest, a steel gray arc with three full moons equidistance above it, the larger moon over the arc's curve, with the two smaller moons flanking it.

To Hamar's credit, his aides actually appeared to be administrative types. They wore neutral unadorned suits over short stocky frames, and their pale hair bristled on their scalps. Dar followed the motion of their deep-set eyes, protected by heavy folds of skin. He relaxed a bit when he realized that their eyes didn't scan rapidly back-and-forth in the telltale fashion of special forces while they approached. These aides were either well-trained and playing the role of administrative staff, or they were exactly what they seemed. Either way, he was still on alert. They all needed to remain so.

"We welcome you to Ranat," Jenar said, and Hamar closed the distance between them with long confident strides. He stopped mere paces before the greeting party, his aides a few steps behind him.

Dar sniffed at the air several times, turned toward Hamar, then sniffed at the air again. All he could detect was the piercing sweet scent of brilliant blue-green Mora blossoms commingled with the damp musky stench of the nearby lagoon.

"I would not bring my Toori to Mahrain," Hamar said, attempting to maintain a civil tone, which obviously took some effort, as his jaw muscles clenched, then spasmed with tension. "My assistants may be from Andrade II," he continued, "but they are purely administrative, I assure you."

"Of course," Dar said. "I was merely noting the heavy fog, how the scent of Mora blossoms manages to pierce through it."

Hamar looked toward the lagoon, frowned. "The muck must be too thick, as I don't smell them."

"Shall we?" Jenar motioned to the others who had accompanied them to the landing area. They stepped forward. Hamar gestured to his aides to follow. "Yes, I am looking forward to seeing what you have done here. It has been a long time since I've been home to Mahrain, even longer since I've visited Ranat. Too long, perhaps."

"Refreshments first, and then we will all sit down to discuss our official matter," Jenar said, keeping his voice neutral, then gesturing his security staff to lead Hamar and his aides into Ranat's east entrance.

* * *

"Now to the matter at hand," Jenar began, watching while one attendant removed empty trays and cups while another brought in coffee, water, and a platter of local fruits. His brother, Rane, entered the room, bent down to whisper something in his ear, then left.

"The others will be arriving shortly. Then we will begin."

Hamar began to speak, then was cut off with a wave of Dar's hand. He settled into his seat, clasped his hands in his lap, prepared himself to wait.

In a few moments, Iliana, Selene, Cassie, Baron, and Ooli came into the room. Two guards remained at the door, standing on either side. Jenar and Dar stood up, followed by Hamar, as they stepped into the small meeting room.

Baron glared at Hamar, clenched and unclenched his hands. Ooli stroked one of them, and he exhaled deeply, relaxed. Cassie didn't even want to look at her uncle and closed her eyes to envision herself with a blank canvas upon which she could paint anything she desired—including painting her uncle out of existence. She couldn't stop wondering what her life would have been like—what all of their lives would have been like—if Hamar had died instead of his brother, her father. Would her father have killed his own brother? His own wife and children? What sort of monster was he? Even the Toori, she realized, were probably not bad by nature. Hamar had manipulated them as he now attempted to manipulate the people in this room.

Iliana and Selene exchanged thoughts about the oblong table and seating arrangement. They would be able to sit opposite, rather than alongside Hamar, with Dar and Jenar at the head and foot of the table.

Once the new arrivals were seated, Dar, Jenar, and Hamar resumed their seats. While the purpose of these formalities was to create an official tone for the meeting, no one assumed its outcome. Iliana and Selene glanced at Dar, remembering their earlier meeting with him, how there were so many unknowns despite what they planned to accomplish. Hamar may be a rogue satellite, but they were determined to control his orbit.

"We are prepared to listen to your official request and to propose a solution that it is hoped will be agreeable to everyone involved," Jenar began.

He was met with silence, and so continued. "What is the nature of your official request, Hamar?"

Hamar closed his eyes, attempted to still his mind as he had been taught by The Sisterhood. Ironically, he could mindwalk, which necessitated intense focus, but he had never been particularly skilled at the mind-stilling practices which were said to be essential to mind and dream walking. Even now, his discursive thoughts and pungent emotions churned like the tides of Soola. This is a charade, he thought. There was no doubt in anyone's mind as to why they were gathered here. They all knew what he wanted—and what he was prepared to pay for it.

"The Waters of Nyr," he said, extending his arms, palms upward, a gesture he often employed in diplomatic circles to imply being open for dialogue or to signify a humble request. While Hamar had fooled many with his dealings in this quadrant and beyond, no one seated at this table believed he was trustworthy.

"And what of The Waters of Nyr?" Jenar replied, leaning forward slightly.

"I would like access to them." Hamar wet his lips, reached for his cup of water, took a drink.

"For what purpose?" Jenar continued, stealing a quick glance at Dar. Even though he hadn't been on Ranat for any length of time over the past twenty years, Dar had maintained contact, and had resumed his duties upon return. In Jenar's mind, Dar would always be his respected superior and mentor. He had learned much from him while on Haura.

Hamar closed his eyes, bowed his head, then reached out his mind. Yes, they believed he had no inkling of the Waters' inherent purpose, but would he acknowledge this ignorance?

"I have sought The Waters of Nyr for the better part of my adult life. Since the untimely passing of my brother, Bahar, and his wife, Galana, of my own wife and son, I have used all resources at my disposal to locate them . . . to no avail." He paused, looked at Cassie and Baron. "And now that my niece and nephew have been found and returned home. . ."

There was a long silence in the room, punctuated only by the sounds of their commingled breathing.

"Now that the children of my brother have been returned home, I would like to, I would be honored to, welcome them into the family, allow them to assume the full measure of their birthright."

"And how do you perceive this birthright, Hamar?" Jenar fought the urge to delineate it himself, but needed the structure, if not the intent, of protocol to be maintained for their plans to play out successfully.

"Possession of their family home on Mahrain. Considerable funds, which include their father's shares in Trilune, have been held in trust. A position within any of Trilune's subsidiaries, if they so choose." He turned his eyes toward Cassie and Baron, but neither of them would raise their eyes to his. "And my blessings for whichever path they choose—whether it is to honor their parents' choice for mates or to remain single."

Baron and Cassie exchanged mental glances, exclaimed, *Like an arranged marriage?! No way are we doing that. . .*

Then Baron caught himself in mid-thought. Ooli. Had they already been chosen for each other? He frowned. Dar was like their guardian, and had been close to their parents, but both of their parents had died before they were conceived and born, and didn't even know of their existence.

Or had they?

Cassie's thoughts traveled down another path entirely. She sought her mind and heart and revisited the fact that she had never felt any real urges toward someone, male or female, and knew her path was elsewhere. But according to Uncle Hamar, she already had a betrothed. Who could it be? In the way that she knew things, Ooli and Baron were destined to be together. But who had been chosen for her? How could she extricate herself as she knew her life would take another path?

Refocusing their minds on the politics of the moment, Cassie and Baron stared at their hands resting palms-down on the table. Baron slid his to the edge of the table, redirected his pent-up frustrations by gripping it.

"The Waters of Nyr are a sacred trust, as you well know. They are protected—and for good reason. How are we to know that once access is granted, you will honor that trust and not misuse them for personal gain?"

Hamar grimaced, pressed his weight of anger into his hands. "I will honor that trust, of course." He relaxed, leaned back in his chair. "I will humble myself before you now and admit that even though I have sought them and failed, I am still ignorant of their true nature and purpose."

Everyone around the table, with the exception of Hamar, smiled.

"We thank you for your honesty, Hamar. If we are all in agreement, a small demonstration will be held. At that time, you will be granted access—but as a witness only. If those terms are acceptable, we will make arrangements."

Everyone nodded in turn.

"Then there is just one more formality to attend to. If you will have your aides provide the documents to restore and release Casaya's and Baran's property."

"But of course," Hamar said, once again attempting, but failing, to meet Cassie's and Baron's eyes. "It is already done. A gesture of good will. Even if my request would be denied." He smiled at his niece and nephew, and chills swept up their spines. They knew not to make eye contact with him, but even a peripheral glance was enough to make them shiver. They exchanged mental promises to not allow Hamar to ever catch them unaware.

"Then this meeting is adjourned. Please accept our continued hospitality until the demonstration. We trust that your quarters are comfortable and that your needs are being attended to."

"Yes. You have been very gracious despite past circum-stances."

Jenar rose, followed by everyone else in the room. Ooli, Baron, and Cassie were ushered from the room first, followed by Hamar. Iliana, Selene, Dar, and Jenar remained behind to discuss what had transpired and to set the plan in motion. Dar announced that he had already contacted The Sisterhood on Soola, and would leave shortly after dawn to bring Nareli to Ranat.

Chapter 34

It was evening when Dar returned to Ranat with Nareli, one of the Sisterhood who had resumed living on Soola. Fortunately, the worst of storm season had passed, so it had been a brief, and uneventful, journey by starslip.

Ooli was beyond excited to see her. How many times had her bua, Dar, taken her to Soola both as a child and as a young woman? She still had lucid dreams of her brief stays on that storm-tossed moon, a place where dreams often bled into waking life, and where nightmares first began to creep and burrow into her dreams. While a part of Ooli had been relieved that the Sisterhood was not her path, there was a part of her that longed to live among them. On any world. . .

Nareli was older now, even more serene, perhaps, but inner, as well as outer beauty continued to radiate from her pale blue face and obsidian eyes. Her blue-black hair was swept up in a labyrinth of braids decorated with bits of bora and other shells. She was wearing an undyed robe of Mora spider silk and the scent of its blossoms emanated from her.

Ooli smiled at her mua, her mother, and fought the urge to run to embrace her. She knew her father often visited for spiritual solace, and hoped that the two of them were able to share each other.

Nareli held out her arms, and Ooli went to them gratefully, leaning against her mother's chest, listening to the steady beat of her hearts, basking in the rare embrace.

"You have grown, daughter," Nareli said, holding her daughter at arm's length to study her.

"I'm still not as tall as you, though," Ooli smiled, remembering how as a young girl she had thought her mother was the tallest woman she had ever seen, and her father, the tallest man, and yet they were of the same height, heads taller than she.

"The others are waiting," Dar said, nodding to the closed door. He wanted to savor this moment. The three of them together on Ranat. He had imagined a day like this, wanted it to extend beyond the Four Directions, but it was not to be. Each of them had a path to walk, and he was grateful that Ooli's, if not Nareli's, was by his side.

* * *

Neither Baron nor Cassie were prepared for what they learned from Nareli, who, along with Ooli, was going to assist them with The Waters of Nyr. Even though they trusted Dar, Selene, and Iliana, they still didn't understand why they had to put on a demonstration for Hamar. He didn't deserve anything but prison for what he'd done to them, their family, and countless others, but just like back on Haura, tyrants like Hamar often got what they wanted, no matter the cost.

While Nareli told them what to expect, and how it would thwart Hamar's further action, they agreed it was the wisest choice. Still, they wished their first experience with The Waters of Nyr wasn't going to be contaminated by Hamar's presence.

It would take several days before they would be ready for the demonstration, several days where Baron, Cassie, and Ooli lived with Nareli in a very unique cave hidden deep within Ranat. There were other such caves throughout the quadrant, such as the one on T'ar-el, or Sihar Meh Toh, but the existence of this one was known only to a few.

It was here that Cassie was finally able to see what had been missing from her paintings, and where Baron was able to flesh out what had eluded him as well. Even Ooli, who had begun her preparation as a child on Soola, began to make connections where she hadn't noticed them before.

The small system of caves was damp, but not unpleasant, as a stream of fresh air passed through them. Most of the walls were slanted, and bore the undulating grooves and striated branching of flowing water that glistened with small crystalline formations. The cave was coolest by the three openings, but deeper back, it was warmed by a natural hot spring that was partially fed by a small waterfall cascading down the furthest wall. There was a series of small ponds in another chamber, where Mora flowers floated on the surface, their white petals resonating with the ambient light.

But even though there was beauty here, and Ooli, Baron, and Cassie felt safe, there was an energetic undercurrent that tugged and pulled at their core. Once Nareli had walked them through the main cave and the anterooms, they had to sit and rest for awhile.

We're being watched, Cassie said in her mind. Baron and Ooli also felt it.

Yes, Nareli responded. *It is the Nyr who watch you.*

Chapter 35

Mahrain's three moons were luminous in the night sky as Cassie and Baron faced each other, kneeling on sea grass mats before a stone basin. While Ooli stood off to the side, her upper back slightly touching the smooth cavern wall, she glanced at each expectant face before her. Iliana and Selene were seated on opposite ends of the arc of witnesses. Next to Iliana was Dar, and next to Selene, Jenar. Hamar was in the center, flanked by two guards on each side.

Simultaneously, Cassie and Baron closed their eyes, extended their arms to submerge the tips of their fingers, then their entire hands, into the basin.

At first, the water was cool, then the first tendrils of heat began to rise up the length of their arms. Hamar leaned forward at the sound of bubbling water. He wanted to see, had to see what was happening. The guards next to him extended their arms across his chest to restrain him, and he leaned back without complaining. He had waited for this moment for more than half of his life. He wasn't going to risk sabotaging it.

The bowl vibrated as the water rippled and swirled, forming a vortex that tugged at Cassie's and Baron's energetic core. Though the basin was shallow and only half full of The Waters of Nyr, both Cassie and Baron felt as if their entire bodies were submerged beneath the crest of a burgeoning wave. It tugged them deep beneath the surface, then cast them over an immense swell.

As their breathing quickened, Ooli stepped forward, resting one hand on each of their shoulders, holding the space, completing the circuit so that they were drawn further into the vortex.

But within this seeming chaos was a calm center, where Cassie, Baron, and Ooli could see through each others eyes, could feel through each others bodies, could completely be in each others thoughts. Their combined sight was magnified exponentially as Ooli reached her hands into the basin, and the three of them interlaced their fingers, hands, and wrists

The air surrounding them was charged with electricity; tendrils of green fire snaked out toward the others. Hamar gasped, leaned forward to rise, and the guards restrained him. He was so enthralled that he barely noticed, and didn't attempt to shake them free. What did the waters do? He asked himself. What *could* they do?

While still kneeling on the brilliant blue sea grass mats, their eyes closed, the portals to other dimensions undulated around them. All three were aware that they were poised at the precipice of an interstitial space, where all possibilities existed.

Where the paths to these possibilities co-existed alongside those that did not exist.

In absolute synchronicity, they opened completely to each other.

There, they thought as one, stepping through the gateway, whorls of pearlescent mist encasing them like the inside of a **boora** shell.

* * *

Hamar yelled "No!" as he jumped out of his seat after Cassie, Baron, and Ooli collapsed, their bodies sprawled at odd angles on the cave floor. The guards placed Hamar in a lock, his arms behind him. Their immense hands clenched a shoulder and elbow as they half-drug, half-carried Hamar from the cave. He struggled against the restraint, angry sweat pouring down his face and neck, trying to crane his neck around to see whether the three still lived. He had not expected this, not expected it at all.

"They still breathe," Iliana and Selene called out, each checking and rechecking Ooli's, Cassie's, and Baron's pulses.

This seemed to satisfy Hamar, and he stopped struggling. The guards released their hold on him. One said, "Keep walking." Hamar did as he was told.

The others listened as the guards' and Hamar's footsteps receded down the corridor before speaking. Selene and Iliana rested their hands on Ooli's, Baron's, and Cassie's foreheads for a few moments, then stroked their hair.

"Nareli was right," Dar began. "Their bodies are here, but their minds. . ." his voice trailed off.

"Their minds are safe, Dar," Selene said, resting a hand over his, looking into his eyes. "Their minds are safe."

He nodded, looked at his daughter, the children of his friends, and sighed, wondering where they wandered, what they were seeing, how it would impact their commingled lives. For the Waters of Nyr weren't exactly fluid water. The Nyr were crystalline beings that lived within special streams of water, and now lived within Cassie, Ooli, and Baron.

Had chosen to live within them.

Chapter 36

With Cassie, Baron, and Ooli now safely on Soola with the Nareli and the Sisterhood, Hamar, believing they were all dead, was beyond rage.

After the demonstration, he was escorted into protective custody, with a specific mandate that no one, absolutely no one, would speak with him until he had regained his composure.

"We all grieve their loss," Iliana said, and this was echoed by Selene and the others.

It was several days before the guards reported that Hamar, who had consistently refused anything but water, seemed sufficiently subdued to engage in a rational dialogue.

"How could you allow them to use The Waters of Nyr if you knew this would happen," he screamed at Dar.

"Contain yourself or I will leave," Dar replied, his guards at attention.

Hamar whirled around to face the wall, clenched and unclenched his fists, fueling, rather than dispelling his rage. A few moments passed, and Dar realized, perhaps before Hamar did, that he was calmer, but his anger seethed beneath the surface.

"Do you not feel any sorrow, any grief, for your niece and nephew?" Dar began. "For *my* daughter."

Hamar turned around to face Dar, studied his old friend's face, nodded. "Please, let us sit and talk." He gestured to one of several benches in the locker room where he was being temporarily jailed. Various types of submersion suits hung on one wall above a series of shelves and bins holding breathers and other diving equipment. Just beyond this area, there were several anterooms; one was filled with cots, another with a bathroom, the third with a large multi-head shower stall that had two combined entrances and exits, one to this room, the other to a corridor which Hamar hadn't explored yet.

"It is a great loss," Hamar continued. "My anger is, of course, the result of this, this, unfortunate event." He bowed his head for a moment, his voice a whisper. "I, too, am no stranger to loss. My wife. My son. Dead. Both dead."

"At whose hand," Dar whispered back.

Hamar jerked toward him, his rage resurfacing with such force that his veins stood out, striating along his forehead.

"You think I did it? That I would take the lives of my own wife, my own son?"

"And of your own brother, his wife, and countless others." Dar said without raising his voice. "We are alone here, Hamar. No one but you and me. The guards are outside and cannot hear us."

"What is it that you would have me say? Admit guilt? That's preposterous."

"And yet you do not deny it. Not convincingly. What did you think you would accomplish if you were able to acquire the Waters of Nyr? If Cassie, Baron, and Ooli had not died in the process?"

Hamar shook his head. "They belong to me. They are my lineage. Mine." His eyes elongated into narrow slits, and Dar was chilled by their ferocity.

"And I, with my lineage, am sworn to protect them, to see that they do not fall into undeserving hands."

Hamar clasped his hands over his knees, and Dar saw how they trembled, saw how Hamar wanted to strike out at him, but was still able to maintain a modicum of composure.

"You are making a mistake, my friend. A huge mistake."

"No, it is you who have made the mistake, old friend. And you will make no more."

And then Dar called out for the guards.

"Your aides will be allowed to contact your vessel as to what has transpired here, to return to that vessel if they so choose. Meanwhile, I suggest you delve deep, Hamar, to consider your current options."

Dar whisked around, left the room, sealing the door behind him.

Chapter 37

If Hamar had known how well-trained the guards were, he would have realized that he had been allowed to escape. After Dar left, he walked the length of the locker room, sat on a cot, tried to lie down, got back up again, paced some more.

And then he remembered the corridor leading away from the showers.

Hamar took his shoes off, padded into the corridor, realized that the musky scent he had detected earlier, grew stronger the further he walked. This had to lead to a grotto, he realized, then returned to the area where the submersion suits were hung. He tried on several before he realized that none would fit his frame. No matter, all he needed was a breather. While he hadn't been in the water for quite some time, he had always been a decent swimmer. He found one that fit, tucked it into his pants, then returned to the corridor's mouth.

This was a Mahrain tunnel, he realized, as the corridor curved left, then right, then circled around before veering off to the side. Hamar had no idea which direction he was walking in, but even though Ranat's architects had obviously kept them in mind when they constructed the station, the Mahrain were sea-dwelling creatures. The tunnel had to lead to open water at some point.

The temperature climbed as Hamar continued at a slow place. He paused to take off his jacket, wrapped it around his waist. He walked a bit further then paused again. What if he were being followed? He reached out with his mind to see if the guards realized he was gone, but didn't see or sense anything. *This is almost too easy,* he thought, then managed a raspy laugh, believing that Ranat had grown sloppy with its emphasis on research. Their security crew was no match for his well-honed evasive skills.

Beads of moisture dripped onto Hamar's head as he con-tinued at an accelerated pace, and was then rewarded with a draft of fresher air. He took a few tentative steps toward an opening, peered out into a small grotto, where water lapped over a bright blue coral bed and series of tidepools. *No one in sight.*

Hamar sat down just inside the tunnel, braced himself along the sides to peer over the lip. He was higher up than he would like, but it was manageable. He eased to the edge and dropped down onto the rock, sliding a bit on the slimy surface.

If he was careful, he wouldn't slip again, he cautioned himself, testing his footing with each step. Occasionally, he would look into the tide pools, remembering how he loved to visit these as a boy with his brother, Bahar. Bahar. . .He allowed himself a moment of regret, then watched it seep into his subconscious like seafoam into the sand.

Hamar crouched down to inspect a small tide pool, saw polyps wriggling free of a piece of pale red coral. There was also an infant nara, brilliant blue, and covered with bits of quartz sand. He remembered how mesmerizing it had been to watch these little microcosms of the universe. Sighing, he stood up reluctantly to make his way toward an opening in the rock which he believed lead closer to the surface.

He sniffed at the air, detected a faint perfume rising above the pungent air. Moora blossoms. Yes, he was close to the surface. And freedom.

Hamar stepped carefully over a series of small tide pools, then around a larger one, until he was finally there. It was a narrow passage, but if he edged around with his back to the wall, there was more than enough room to squeeze between the sheaths of rock.

He checked the gauge on the breather again. There was more than enough air. He had grabbed a pair of goggles as an afterthought, and was relieved that they fit, even though they were a bit tight. He took off his shirt and thought about remov-ing his pants as well, but decided against that. While he didn't want any extraneous clothes to weigh him down, he also didn't want to be caught totally naked once he reached the surface.

Dressed only in Trilune-issue pants that clung to his legs, he braced himself, dove into the water, and was surprised at its unusual warmth.

Another good sign, he thought. Escape was imminent. He was confident that his assistant had been successful in working the code for immediate departure into the single communiqué he was allowed. The cruiser would be waiting for him. The Trilune vessel would still be hovering above Ranat. He would deal with the political repercussions of his escape at another time. Dar couldn't prove that he had poisoned his family. There were no witnesses left.

The water wasn't as dark as expected, and Hamar wondered at that for a moment until he saw a school of *toolas* swimming back and forth, their heads surrounded with irides-cent filaments that alternately glowed brilliant orange, red, then golden yellow. It was a beautiful sight. He couldn't remember the last time he had been so close to these intriguing creatures. He had been spending too much time engaged in official business and trying to maintain knowledge as to the where-abouts of his niece and nephew—and The Waters of Nyr. Now he was certain that the coveted substance had been on Sihar Meh Toh all along, that the Sisterhood had something to do with protecting it. He was not blind. . .He'd seen the blue-skinned witch with Dar. Why else would one of them be on Mahrain now? The team he'd sent to T'arla must have lied to him. Or else they were like Poochi larva and blind to what was right in front of their eyes the entire time.

Hamar made a mental note to call the last team in for questioning. Who had headed it again? Ah yes, Barto. He had been loyal to Trilune, but was no longer in its employ. Who to send out next time? He needed to think that through in more detail during the trip to his current home on Tyraelia.

With thoughts focused more on the future than the present moment, Hamar swam through a field of undulating sea grass until he came upon several openings in an outcropping of rock. He had been careful to follow the ridge as he swam. He checked inside one opening. It appeared to be too narrow. The next one was blocked with tangled sea grass and the skeletal remains of some poor creature. The last one, which canted upward, was the best choice. It was more than wide enough for him to swim through, and he could see the bobbing of bright patches of light just beyond its opening.

This is the one, he told himself, easing through.

It was a short tunnel, just as he had hoped. He was almost there, almost to the surface.

Hamar attempted to settle on a rock to re-adjust his goggles and the breather, treading water to keep himself upright. The current was barely perceptible, which he didn't question, especially since he was just below the surface. Just a few flutter kicks and he would be breathing fresh air.

He raised his arms, kicked off. He did it again to no avail, realized his foot was stuck.

When Hamar bent down, there was a tangle of sea grass interspersed with pale blue filaments that writhed between the clumped grass. He tugged, and had almost released his foot when he felt a tug on his other foot. He bent to extract that one, struggled as he realized he was standing in a huge bed of the grass. Where had this come from? He hadn't noticed it before.

Thinkthinkthink, he urged himself, wishing he had a blade to slice through it. There was still more than enough air in the breather. He should just relax a moment. No need to panic.

And then excruciating pain sliced through his body. After it slightly dissipated, Hamar attempted to writhe free. Eyes clenched and hyperventilating through the breather, he realized that he would pass out if he didn't calm down. Coral. He had probably scraped his foot on a piece of coral. That was it.

He felt woozy, but even so, he was able to release some of the tangles around his ankle and calf. He hadn't realized how prevalent the grass would be so close to the surface.

And then a proboscis snaked out, wrapping itself around his left arm. Confused, he reached over, slipped his fingers under it, tried to tear it away, blood clouding around him.

Another proboscis snaked out, knocked the breather off his face. Then another and another, wrapping around his other arm, his head and neck, then torso.

In the aquarium's observation deck, Dar and Jenar watched silently as Hamar ceased to struggle. The pod of naras tore him into chunks, rivulets of blood and gore clouding the clear water.

The naras wouldn't need to feed again for quite some time.

Epilogue

With Hamar and his Toori no longer a threat, Baron and Cassie began to adjust to the rhythm of their new lives on Mahrain. This included moving into their family home, which Baron was relieved to discover was mostly above ground. Their Muas Iliana and Selena agreed to live with them until they were situated, but Baron and Cassie promised that it would be quite some time before they wanted to be on their own.

Ooli was a frequent visitor, as was Jenar, who was doing his best not to be too obvious about his interest in Cassie, or Casaya, as he still insisted on calling her. He agreed with Cassie that betrothals were a thing of the past—even on Mahrain—but had been pleasantly surprised to discover that he had real feelings for her, feelings that weren't manufactured from obligation.

Dar would often stop by for tea or supper, and while talk did occasionally turn toward Baron's, Cassie's, and Ooli's further training, everyone decided they deserved some time to just be.

The Nyr agreed.

Glossary

Andrade II (An-dra-dee): An unofficial Marainian moon with Trilune mining interests.

Bejar (Be-zhar): One of Mahrain's three official moons.

Boora Shell: The outside of this shell has razor-sharp protrusions to protect the creature inside which resembles a Hauran clam. The inside of the shell is similar to that of a Hauran abalone, pearlescent with varying shades of purple.

Boort (Bore-t): A term used to designate a particular group of planets that are economically, politically, and otherwise connected; 2. dialectically, it also translates as "home".

Bua (boo-a): Father.

Haura: Earth, located in The Milky Way galaxy.

Kham: A humanoid species of shapeshifters who bear no resemblance to the Toori. They are believed to be indigenous to Psion IV, where mining colonies currently exist. They are able to shift between forms and maintain them for a long duration. More adaptable.

Mahrain: 1. A planet in the Boortean galaxy; 2. a giant sea eel indigenous to Mahrain's Mora Sea, for which the planet is named; 3. a constellation that resembles the sea eel.

Mindspeed: Literally, the speed of thought.

Moodies: slang for a unit of time; a nanosecond.

Mora (moora): Includes various species of Mahrainian flowers, some of which are aquatic and thrive in wetlands, lagoons, or on the banks of isolated bodies of water. Other varieties grow in mountain areas. Hues include bright blue, fuchsia, and ivory.

Mora Sea: One of two major bodies of water located on Mahrain.

Mora Spider: A deadly spider that camouflages itself as the center of the Mora blossom, its spindly legs jutting out to cover the blossoms. Its silk is woven into garments and other fabrics, and its venom has psychotropic properties and is also used as medicine and has been known to poison people—both intentionally as well as unintentionally.

Mua (moo-a): mother.

Nara: An aquatic creature indigenous to the Mora Sea on Mahrain.

Nua (noo-a): Aunt.

Nyr (neer): Crystal beings with immense powers and knowledge. They are aligned with The Sisterhood as well as the T'ar-el, and may choose to bond, integrate, or share consciousness with others. They do not need to exist in a symbiotic relationship with a host body, but may choose to do so. They usually live within subterranean cavers such as those on Mahrain and Sihar Meh Toh.

P1: Mahrainin station on Poora, one of Mahrain's three official moons.

Poochi Bug: A type of honey-making "insect" (for want of a better category) that flies but can also maneuver on—and in—the ground. They are most prevalent in the steppes near inactive volcanoes. Their tiered hives can range in height from a few feet to over twenty-feet. Circumferences range in size as well. It is believed that certain types of Poochi Bugs burrow miles beneath the ground. They are considered to be poisonous to most humanoid species. The Poochi Bug and its behavior is a rich source of metaphor in the Boortean lexicon.

Psion IV (sy-on): A small unofficial moon where there is a mining colony. The indigenous home, it is believed, of Kham shapeshifters, before Trilune and other transgalactic interests colonized it.

Pua (poo-a): 1. Infant or baby; tadpole, or the newly-hatched offspring of a Pua-Pua, indigenous to the Mora Sea; 2. Shooting star.

Pua-Pua (poo-a-poo-a): An bottom dwelling aquatic creature that moves exceptionally fast on its spindly legs and elongated body.

Ranat (ra-naat): Under-water space facility on Mahrain, located in the Mora Sea.

Sihar Meh Toh (she-har-meh-toh): The Rim of Sorrows; the lunar home of the T'ar-el, a species of shape-shifters, as well as the Nyr. Due to it's being considered off-limits, it is not included in the official registry of Mahrain's moons.

Sisterhood: Also known as Sisters of the Blood Moon.

Soola: One of Mahrain's three official moons, and home to the Sisters of the Blood Moon.

Sozar (So-zharr): 1. An expletive like "awesome"; 2. a swear word (depending upon tone); 3. said as a toast and/or to congratulate someone; and 4. something said in frustration.

Star Gazer Café: A café that is also a Mahrainian safehouse.

Sua (soo-a) sister.

Synthsuits: A bio-engineered "synthetic" skin worn by Boorteans to appear human. It is not a suit in the usual sense of the word as it can be carried in a small pouch, but once it makes contact with its wearer, the individual particles will follow their programming and cover the individual with an impenetrable form that looks and behaves like the skin of a specific species. Not to be confused with Xenosynth™ models, which are actual synthetic beings programmed to fulfill specific functions.

T'ar-el (Ta-ar-el): Also known as The Guardians, these shape-shifting beings inhabit Sihar Meh Toh, The Rim of Sorrows, a supposedly barren moon.

T'arla (Ti-ar-la): Also referred to as The Rim of Sorrows and Sihar Meh Toh. An icy planet thought to be abandoned, but which is home to the T'ar-el, a shape-shifting species.

Tau (tah-oo): son

T'bua (ta-boo-a): Grandfather.

The Four Corners: 1. The four directions of the galaxy that expand in all directions: east, west, south, and north; 2. A reference to mind expansion; 3. A reference to "loosing" ones mind; and 4. A video rental and sales store on Haura that is also a Mahrainian safe house.

T'mua (ta-moo-a): Grandmother.

Toola: One of Mahrain's moons.

Toori (too-ree): One of several shape-shifting species. While humanoid, they have four-to-six arms, and tentacle-like upper appendages. Their skin tone is usually a pale yellow, rubbery, and hangs down in folds.

Tua (too-a): Daughter.

Transport Dizzy Flu: A condition that ensues when someone has a physiological reaction to a variety of transport modalities, specifically the Boortean equivalent of the well-known *Star Trek* transportation method known as "Beam-me-up-Scottie-time". A physics professor known to the author actually referred to it within several lectures as an aid to assist her in understanding a variety of concepts which seem oh-so-much-clearer to the less mathematically-challenged.

Trilune IV: One of Trilune's operation bases located on Psion V.

Tyraelia: A cold, desert-like planet, with three moons.

Waters of Nyr: 1. A mythological stream of water believed to contain miraculous medical properties; 2. An actual stream or body of water where the Nyr, a powerful sentient lifeform, live. This water is imbued with various elements and properties that enable other beings to share consciousness, shift through time and space, and as the legend states, heal all ills. However, if the Waters of Nyr fall into the wrong hands, death, madness, and other catastrophes may occur.

www.ingramcontent.com/pod-product-compliance
Lightning Source LLC
LaVergne TN
LVHW012331100826
845148LV00017B/2107

* 9 7 8 0 9 8 2 8 9 7 5 1 5 *